This book is to be returned on or before
the last date stamped below.

Also by the same author:

Flip Side
Trillions

MINDBENDERS

17156/F

Nicholas Fisk

Hodder
Children's
Books

a division of Hodder Headline plc

Copyright © 1987 Nicholas Fisk

First published in Great Britain in 1987
by Penguin Books Ltd.

This edition published in Great Britain in 1998
by Hodder Children's Books

The right of Nicholas Fisk to be identified as the Author of the
Work has been asserted by him in accordance with
the Copyright, Designs and Patents Act 1988.

10 9 8 7 6 5 4 3 2 1

A Catalogue record for this book is
available from the British Library

ISBN 0340 71020 9

Typeset by
Palimpsest Book Production Limited

Printed and bound in Great Britain by
Clays Ltd, St Ives plc

Hodder Children's Books
A Division of Hodder Headline plc
338 Euston Road
London NW1 3BH

Just before things got really serious—
at the time when Vinny and Toby had mastered their minds—
but before they knew what they were getting into—
this happened . . .

Chapter One

Vinny said, 'No, don't, we mustn't, it's cruel, it's mean.'

But her brother Toby saw the corners of her mouth twitch. 'Ah, come on,' he said. 'Do old Bloggs good. Wake him up.'

They were upstairs looking out of the window and down on the garden. It was sunny, hot. Bloggs lay on his favourite paving stone, legs stretched, golden eyes narrowed to slits. Happy fat black cat.

'Look at his bulging belly!' Toby said. 'Middle-age spread. He needs exercise. We'd be doing him a favour.'

'He's not middle-aged,' Vinny said.

'He is. You're nine, he's ten, I'm eleven. Bang in the middle.'

'Ten's not middle-aged for a cat,' Vinny said. She stared worriedly at Bloggs. You multiply a cat's age by seven, or is it five? Either way, she thought, I suppose Bloggs is getting middle-aged. How sad.

At that moment, Bloggs rolled over and lay on his back, with limp front paws dangling over his chest and his rear legs stretched out rigidly, like stilts. Even at this distance, you could see the smirk on his face. Vinny had to smile, then laugh.

'Go on!' Toby insisted.

'Well . . .' she said. The frown came back to her face, but a different frown, a frown of intense concentration. Her dark eyes became black, her lower lip pouted. '*Little brown mouse . . .*' she murmured.

'Terrific, that's it, keep at it!' Toby whispered.

'*Little brown mouse, little brown mouse!*' Vinny repeated. And there it was: a little brown mouse, sleek and plump! It sat on its haunches almost in front of Bloggs's nose. Its whiskers vibrated. it washed itself.

'Great, terrific, brill, genius!' Toby murmured.

At first, Bloggs saw nothing, he was too busy enjoying the sun. But then he rolled over, yawning – and glimpsed something small, brown, glossy and plump. A mouse! A mouth-watering, succulent mouse!

His sun-bathing position became a stalking crouch. His chin touched the warm paving stone. His shoulder-blades made two devilish humps, higher than his head. The tip of his tail twitched.

The mouse washed behind its ears with paws that moved as fast as an electric buzzer.

Bloggs crawled forward on his belly, a centimetre at a time.

The mouse kept washing itself.

Vinny bit her lip and stared, fascinated.

Bloggs was within springing distance.

Toby rubbed his hands and stared, wide-eyed.

Bloggs bunched his muscles. He had only to spring, claws spread, hooked teeth ready to crunch shut—

'*Cancel!*' Vinny shouted

And suddenly, there was no mouse.

Instantly, Bloggs changed from mighty hunter to puzzled pussycat. He sniffed at the place where the mouse had been. He even patted the place with his paw. He raised his head and gave a complaining 'Miaow!' No mouse.

'Oh!' cried Vinny, melodramatically, 'Oh, how mean! How rotten we are! How awful! Oh, poor Bloggs!'

'Don't drivel,' Toby said. 'It was a fantastic success. You're getting better every day.'

'That's true,' Vinny said, forgetting the dramatics. 'I am getting good. Of course, you helped. I can't do it alone.'

'I don't think I help all that much. I mean, I concentrate like mad and try and make rays of thought come out of my eyes and all that. But it's still you.'

'Me and you – and the ants,' Vinny said, slowly. 'Don't ever forget the ants. They changed everything.'

'If you're going to get all mystical,' Toby began.

'But it is all mystical!' Vinny said. 'That was a Mystical Mouse!'

Toby did not answer. He bit his lip for a little while, then said, 'You say things have changed. When? How? What?'

They were in the bedroom they used to share when they were little. Now it was Toby's room and a mess. To find a place to sit down, Vinny had to push things aside with her foot – bicycle chainwheels, magazines, a busted computer, DM boots, pyjamas. 'You really are a filthy pig,' she said, but her heart wasn't in the remark. Like Toby, she was thinking deeply about the Mystical Mouse and other amazing things. Unexplainable things.

They sat thinking. 'Absolutely filthy,' Vinny said vaguely. Then – 'Let's start at the beginning,' she said. 'Let's find out what we are and who we are and what we're doing.'

'Frodsham's Fun Book,' Toby said. 'That was where it began. "Why is a race horse like an ice-cream? Because the more you lick it, the faster it goes."'

'Ha, *ha*,' Vinny said, hollowly.

'"Barber to Customer: 'My goodness, sir, your hair is getting thin!' Customer to Barber: 'Who wants fat hair?'"'

'Ho, ho, ho,' Toby said, mournfully. 'To think we once laughed.'

'We were young, then,' Vinny said. 'Just jolly little toddlers. Grotty old *Frodsham's Fun Book* . . . all those blurry drawings and optical illusions and card tricks and everything . . .'

'And "How to Amaze Your Friends",' Toby said. '"100 Mystifying Tricks that Any Bright Youngster Can Learn".'

'The Sealed-Envelope Mind-reading Trick,' Vinny said. 'Remember that? Good, that was. So simple, but nobody ever saw through it.'

They laughed at the memory. Card tricks, mental tricks, conjuring tricks – they had learned them all. The mystical tricks went down best. People *wanted* to believe the mystical impossible, they discovered.

But then everyone became older. The old tricks no longer thrilled and mystified. Vinny and Toby grew tired of being magicians. More interesting things came up: computers, video games, BMX bikes, camping holidays, all sorts of things. Yet the glamour of the old days, when Toby and Vinny had Amazed their Friends, still lingered on.

All at once, magic was back in fashion. The TV, particularly, was full of magic. A British magician made impossible feats look easy, week after week. In America, a magician made a complete airliner disappear, then the Statue of Liberty. Vinny and Toby saw it happen on the gogglebox.

'Wow!' Vinny said, switching off the TV. 'The things they're doing nowadays! Perhaps we ought to start again. But we'd have to find something really unusual, really *interesting*. I mean, like that man who bent spoons and stopped clocks.'

Toby said, 'We only know about him because Dad put him on video. Everyone else has forgotten him.'

'Maybe. But his *act* – mental powers and all that – it's better than plain conjuring. Bending spoons and stopping clocks and everything. Mystical powers. *Mindbending*. If we could let people see something like that—'

'They just *thought* they saw. Really, there was nothing to see. It was all in the mind.'

'But that's just what I'm saying. I bet if we practised enough, we could do mind tricks. You know, willing to make things move. Or knowing which card would be dealt next.'

'The only thing you could do with *your* mind,' Toby said, 'is stop a clock. Or perhaps your face would do it better.'

'Don't be childish,' Vinny said, primly. She did not want to argue. Something told her that there was more to Mental Magic than clever conjuring. But she did not yet know what that something might be.

Then Aunt Craven came to stay.

Aunt Craven's visits, like Christmas, didn't occur often, but they stayed in the mind. Again like Christmas, you could feel the tension building up before the event.

Toby's and Vinny's mother, Bets, suffered most from the tension. You could tell that she was frightened of her older sister, Craven, by the way she fussed over everything.

'Mum's cooking again!' Toby told Vinny.

'Not *again*,' Vinny replied. 'She'll burst the freezer! What's she cooking now?'

'One of those crummy cakes, the health-food ones,' Toby said. 'You know, all bran and roughage and free-range sultanas. Real Aunt Craven cake.'

Vinny made a groaning noise. 'So we're going to have to eat vegetarian muck,' she said. 'No meat, no white bread, no buttered crumpets—'

'It's the wrong time of year for crumpets,' Toby said. 'Still, I see what you mean. I *hate* pure food made from natural ingredients.'

'I hate Aunt Craven,' Vinny said. 'Bullying Mum, dominating everything, making us eat horrible food.'

Toby said, 'Look at old Bloggs! Even he knows Aunt Craven's coming!' Bloggs was standing in the doorway, looking humpy and embarrassed. He didn't seem to know where to put himself. He said, 'M-roop?' in a miserable sort of voice. Vinny picked him up, but he felt awkward and his hind legs stuck out like furry sticks.

'Poor old Bloggs,' Vinny said. 'You know she's coming, don't you? And soon she'll be here, and you'll be disapproved of and have to lurk about in the garden.'

Toby said, 'It's funny how cats and dogs know things. There's Mental Magic for you!' He leaned out of the window, trying to see the road through the trees and shrubs that encircled the house, cutting it off from the neighbours. 'No sign of her yet,' he reported.

Then – 'Oh-oh! Here comes trouble!'

He'd spotted Aunt Craven's Daimler Conquest.

Vinny spilled Bloggs from her lap and joined Toby at the window. 'Same old Daimler!' she whispered. She did not have to whisper, but she did.

'Smoking worse than ever!' Toby grinned. 'And that front wheel looks a bit umpty. It's got a wobble.'

The solid, bulbous, convertible car, a relic of the 1950s, ponderously grunched to a halt. Aunt Craven switched off the engine, but the engine did not stop. It ran on, going, 'Boo-boo-BOOMP, boo-boo-boo-BOOMP, boo-boo-BANG!' Toby grinned. The BANG! had been a real shatterer. 'Bet that blew the exhaust!' he said, happily.

The driver's door opened and Aunt Craven got out. She was scowling. The BANG! had upset her. She went to the back of the car and wrenched at the boot's handle. It came off in her hand.

'"Don't believe in your modern tinware,"' Toby whispered in Vinny's ear. She giggled.

'"Old-style British craftsmanship is good enough for me,"' she whispered back. They could both imitate Aunt Craven's voice perfectly.

They watched Aunt Craven fiddle with the boot handle – get it back and working again – and tug cases out. She had a lot of luggage, as usual.

'She hasn't seen us,' Vinny said.

But at that moment, Aunt Craven bawled, 'Toby!

Vinny! I can see you! Come down here and lend us a hand with this lot!'

Bloggs hid under the bed, and Toby and Vinny went downstairs, pulling faces at each other and tidying their clothes.

After they'd lugged all the luggage into the hall, they entered the living-room: Vinny a dear little girlie with wide, innocent eyes and Toby a fine, manly young fellow with an open countenance. His hands were filthy, so he kept them behind his back.

Their mother, Bets, had a smile on her face. It was what Toby and Vinny called her Loony Smile, the fixed smile that meant she was thoroughly ill at ease. 'Oh, *there* you are,' Bets said, as if her children had been missing for three weeks. 'Say hallo properly to Aunt Craven!'

'Hallo, Aunt Craven,' Vinny said, girlishly.

'Hallo, Aunt Craven,' Toby said, manfully.

'Hah!' Aunt Craven barked. There was a short silence until Aunt Craven added, 'Your shirt's hanging out.' Toby flinched and tucked his shirt in, remembering too late about his dirty hands: she'd spot them. He thought, Round One to Aunt Craven.

'Aunt Craven's staying four whole days!' Bets said, her voice about fifty per cent too enthusiastic. Vinny thought, She's been at the sherry. Don't blame her.

Another silence fell. Toby and Vinny studied Aunt Craven. She was both like and unlike her sister Bets. Both were solidly built, with neat arms and legs. Both

9

had curling dark hair, round faces and noticeable dark eyes. But where Bets's eyes glowed, Aunt Craven's glared. Where Bet's arms looked as if they might be good at cuddling small children, Aunt Craven's somehow suggested unarmed combat. Where Bets's hair looked as if it might be a bit difficult to style and cut, Aunt Craven's seemed to say, 'Go on scissors – I dare you!'

Aunt Craven broke the silence. 'Hands could do with a wash,' she announced, staring at Toby. 'But that can come after you've fixed my Daimler's boot handle. Suitable nail – hacksaw – tap with a hammer. Nothing to it, right?'

For a moment, Toby was thrown. Then, a sidelong glance showed him Vinny's face and eyes: the face like a party jelly, sweet and nice and shiny and soft. But her eyes were shiny and hard. They were fixed on Aunt Craven's hands. Toby stared at them too.

Unwinking, they stared at Aunt Craven's hands, Letting the silence build. The fingers of the right hand were stained a bright orange-brown. Smoker's fingers.

They stared until Aunt Craven cracked. She pretended to smooth her skirt – and hid the tell-tale hand behind her.

Round Two to us, thought Toby. He said, 'My *hands* are dirty, you're quite right, Aunt Craven. I'll go and wash my *hands*, Mum.'

'Ooo, yes, wash your *hands*!' Vinny cooed.

They left the room, went upstairs to the bathroom and closed the door. 'Ciggies!' Toby said. 'Her one and only weakness. Still puffing away, in spite of all her pure food and organically grown veg. Bossy as ever, of course – but she's got her one weak spot.' He washed his hands, smoothed his hair and adjusted his collar. The mirror showed him a noble British boy.

'We'll have her guts for garters,' Vinny replied. She looked more than ever the perfect English rosebud.

Both of them knew, from long experience, the value of relatives. Their affectionate Auntie Vi, suitably prodded, produced whole-nut milk chocolate till the cows came home. Uncle Fred, if you kept him talking about his Jaguar, could be milked of 50p pieces – even £s. Uncle Vic, the Cost Accountant, could be relied on for small change if only you let him keep telling you all about the vital role of the Cost Accountant in commerce.

All you had to do with the relations was handle them skilfully. 'But Aunt Craven's different,' Vinny said. 'She handles us. She handles everyone. Old Bossyboots.'

'Dead right,' Toby said. 'Booming Bossyboots. She's got to be smashed down. Made to submit – you know, Vin, like they do in all-in wrestling. Ow! Moan, groan, I submit!'

Bloggs entered the room. Toby grabbed him and said, '*Submit!*' Bloggs said, 'Mrrps,' blinked and rolled over on his back.

'Aunt Craven won't be as easy as Bloggs,' Vinny said.

They went to Toby's room to make plans.

* * *

Somehow, however their conversations started, Vinny and Toby always ended up talking about magic. It was the same this time. Toby was talking about various plans to shatter Aunt Craven. Vinny said, 'Yes, great! Mental Magic! We'd radiate mental death rays at her—'

'Never mind the Mental Magic,' Toby said. 'Our problem is Aunt Craven.'

'No, seriously, we haven't really tried Mental Magic. Well, I suppose we *have* tried – but not hard enough. We give up too easily.'

'If you're talking about trying to make a glass move over a table simply by staring at it—'

Vinny said, 'That's just what I mean. I know we've tried, often. But we ought to try still harder. And when we can make a glass tumbler move, we'll be able to do something horrible to Aunt Craven.'

'If we had some ham, we could have ham and eggs – if we had some eggs,' Toby said, scornfully. 'Look, Vin: Mental Magic is out.'

'But the last time we tried the glass trick, I saw it move! Honestly! Only a little, when your back was turned, but it moved! I'm sure it did!'

'In a pig's eye it moved!' Toby said. 'About Aunt Craven—'

'Let's give it one more try!' Vinny said. 'They're all gassing away at each other down there, we won't be disturbed. Come on, be a sport!'

She went to get a glass. Toby unwillingly helped clear

12

a shiny-topped table. They put the glass in the centre, upside-down. They cupped their chins in their hands. They glared till their eyes watered and their brains fogged. The glass took no notice of them.

At last Toby leaned back, groaned and said, 'I give up.'

'No, don't! Just once more!'

'All right, then,' he said. 'Heads down, eyes glare, *Mindbenders!*' It was their magic incantation. It had never worked. It did not work now.

'Let's pack it in,' Toby said, a long minute later. 'It's never going to work.'

'Just one more go!'

'You know what the trouble is!' Toby said. 'It's lack of voltage, right? We can't make a glass move because it weighs a lot and our minds can't develop enough voltage, enough *power*, to shift it, right?'

'I wish you wouldn't keep saying "right",' Vinny said sniffily.

'But if we directed our minds into the *computer* . . . if we tried to influence a *micro* thing . . . we might succeed. Make it give impossible printouts, or something.'

'Gosh,' Vinny said. 'Wouldn't that be exciting. Excuse my yawn.'

'And I've got another idea, something even more interesting,' Toby said.

'Do tell,' Vinny said, flapping her eyelashes.

'Perhaps the computer will *multiply* what our minds produce! Think of that! The computer could step up our power! Like the coil in a car's electrical circuit, multiplying the battery's voltage from—'

'From 12 volts to 12,000 volts,' Vinny said. She yawned again. 'You've told me all this before. Often.'

'Maybe I have. Sorry, I'm sure. But can't we give it a try?'

Vinny made a disgusted blowing noise, trying to puff the hair off her forehead. 'Oh, all *right*,' she said. 'Come here, computer. Sit in front of me. Attend. You're going to go barmy.'

She propped her head between her hands. Toby did the same. 'Heads down, eyes glare, brains boil,' she said.

'*Mindbenders*!' Toby hissed.

They kept at it for a long time. Nothing happened. The computer refused to go barmy. Two and two still made four. And Aunt Craven still ruled the roost.

Yet, only ten minutes or so later, Toby and Vinny began to fight back against Aunt Craven.

She ran out of ciggies.

'I would be greatly obliged,' she said, 'if one or the other of you would bicycle to the village for me before the shops close.'

'I'll go, Aunt Craven,' Toby said. 'That is, if I haven't got a flat front tyre.'

'I'd go, Aunt Craven,' Vinny said, her face aglow with

anxiety to please, 'only my rotten old *chain* keeps coming off and Daddy thinks it's not safe.'

'I'll make it to the village somehow,' Toby said, manfully. 'What do you want me to get, Aunt Craven?' He knew the answer already, of course, and thoroughly enjoyed watching Aunt Craven force out her answer.

'Just a packet of twenty,' she said. 'But they must be Henson & Badges, understand?'

'Oh, that's right, you *smoke*, don't you, Aunt Craven?' Vinny said, popping her eyes wide open to their Shock-Horror expression. 'Oh, your poor *lungs*. All *black*.'

Aunt Craven gulped but refused to give in. 'Henson & Badges' Original Virginia,' she said, loudly and clearly. 'If the shop does not have them, kindly ask them to lay in a stock.'

'How large a stock?' Vinny asked, politely. 'I mean, are you very heavily addicted?'

'Of course, if I cycled over to Little Frodsham,' Toby said, 'they'd be open there. But I can't trust my front-tyre valve, can I, Vinny?'

'It's all leaky, that valve,' Vinny agreed. 'Fff-sssss!' she added.

'I'd buy a new tyre valve, but I've got no pocket money left,' Toby said.

There was a longish silence. At the end of it, Aunt Craven said, 'What does a new tyre valve cost?'

'Two pounds fifty,' Toby lied, gloomily.

'Isn't that a terrible swizz?' Vinny said. 'All that money for a teeny tiny tyre valve!'

'Here's ten pounds,' Aunt Craven said. 'You'd better keep the change.'

'Oh, thank you, Aunt Craven!' said Toby, and went off on his bike to the village, whistling. Money for old rope.

Chapter Two

It turned out that Aunt Craven was to stay for only three days. Nevertheless, in that short time Toby and Vinny scored the occasional Win.

The tyre valve was, of course, a Win. Even if Toby's bike *had* had a leaky valve, a replacement would have cost him nothing – he had jam jars full of bike bits and spares. So that was one up to Toby and Vinny, definitely.

The next Win came the following evening. There was a magic show on TV. Toby and Vinny wanted to watch it and said so, despite warning glances from Bets and their father, Robbie. Aunt Craven said, 'Pah! *Magic!*' and settled herself in Bets's favourite chair with a pile of magazines.

The magazines were strange-looking. They were badly printed. Blurred pictures on the front covers showed rays of light coming out of people's heads, or people in nighties looking upwards to something fiery in the sky. The nightie people were surrounded by animals, with huge, weepy, gooey eyes. Toby and Vinny tried to see more but couldn't, as the magazines were in a pile, except for one lying flat on Aunt Craven's lap.

Bravely, Vinny switched on the TV. A man was doing a trick. He seemed to know what was in people's minds. 'And the card you are thinking of is the nine of spades, am I right?' he asked.

'Why, yes, it is!' said the lady in the audience. She was amazed. Everyone was.

Aunt Craven said, 'Bah!'

Toby turned down the sound and said, 'You don't believe in magic, do you, Aunt Craven?'

'Load of nonsense,' Aunt Craven replied, without looking up.

'But aren't those magazines to do with spiritualism or mysticism or something?' Toby asked.

'I am interested in things *spiritual*, certainly,' Aunt Craven said. 'But *spiritualism* – certainly not.'

Vinny said, 'But don't spoon-benders put out some sort of spiritual force to bend their spoons?'

Aunt Craven fired up. 'Bunkum! Twaddle!' she exploded. 'Spoon-bending, indeed! If God had intended us to bend spoons, he'd have made us – made us—'

'Spoon-benders?' Toby suggested.

'Rubbish!' Aunt Craven exploded. 'Ghosts and goblins

18

and table-rappers and spoon-benders – all food for fools!' She lit a cigarette so fiercely that its tip glowed like a torch bulb. Her straight back became a ramrod. Her nostrils became twin exhaust pipes.

'So you don't believe in magic?' Toby said. 'Not any sort of magic?'

'I don't discuss my beliefs with urchins,' Aunt Craven said.

'Oh, Aunt Craven! You don't mean *us*?' said Vinny, soulfully.

Aunt Craven made a noise like 'Grrumph' and kept her eyes fixed on her magazine. Toby said, 'But you must believe in some magical things, Aunt Craven! I mean, do you believe in mental powers, if they're organized? Lots of people concentrating on the same thing?'

'I most certainly do,' Aunt Craven said. 'That is the basis of our faith.'

'Our faith?' Toby hinted.

'The Daughters of the Tabernacle,' said Aunt Craven, unwillingly.

'Oo, are you a Daughter?' Vinny cried, popping her eyes girlishly. 'How exciting! And is the Tabernacle something spiritual? And is that its magazine? Oh, do let me look!'

Before Aunt Craven could stop her, Vinny seized several magazines. 'Oh, look, Toby!' she said, pointing to a picture of a lady in an illuminated nightdress holding a baby in one hand and the branch of a tree in the other. 'She's doing magic! Isn't that lovely! And look at this dear little fawn with its great big shiny eyes! And this *camel* . . . such a kind face!'

Toby nudged Vinny to say, 'You're overcooking it!' Aunt Craven remained stone-faced. Vinny rattled on.

'Oh, and here's another lady! Wow, her feet are *inches* off the ground, she's sort of floating on nothing! And making flames all around her! I suppose she just floats about wherever she likes, how lovely for her! More magic!'

'She is *not* doing magic,' Aunt Craven began. At that moment, Bets popped her over-bright face round the door and said, 'Supper time!' So the game of Auntbaiting had to be dropped.

But not entirely. When Vinny came to her grapefruit, she made a face and said, 'Poo! It's so sour!' Then, turning her bright and innocent face to Aunt Craven, she said, 'Do you suppose, Auntie, that if *lots* and *lots* of Daughters of the Tabernacle *all* prayed at the same time for my grapefruit to be sweet, that it *would* be sweet?'

Watching his aunt's furious face, Toby thought, magic! Pure magic!

Aunt Craven's farewell gifts, when she left at the end of her three-days' stay, were typically insulting. To Bets and Robbie, she gave a bottle of cheap sweet sherry. 'I know you two like a tipple,' she said. 'Can't stand the stuff myself. Poison. Muck. Still, if it's what you like . . .'

For Vinny and Toby she bought a formicarium: a nest of ants, a complete colony, in a flat wooden box with a glass cover. A feeding tube stuck out of the side. She got it from the Back-to-Nature commune outside the village. The men had beards, the women wore layers of sweaters and the children had runny noses. They were quite popular. 'It all sounds a bit daft, that commune,' people said, 'but they're probably right, you know.'

'Here you are, you two, a *present*,' Aunt Craven barked. 'A *formicarium*. Cop hold. No, not like that! Hold it steady! Ants have feelings. More feelings than some people I know.'

'Say "Thank you, Aunt Craven,"' Bets said, feebly. Toby and Vinny muttered their thanks, but Aunt Craven didn't listen. 'I hope you'll *learn* something from these little creatures,' she said. 'You and your computers and your magic! What you have here is a living computer, a living piece of magic, made not by the feeble hand of Man, but by the all-powerful hand of—'

'Thank you, Aunt Craven. It's very nice.'

'Thank you, Aunt Craven. It's ever so lovely.'

'*Nice! Lovely!*' Aunt Craven said, scornfully. Under her breath, she muttered something about illiterate cretins.

She got into her Daimler. Its massive door slammed shut with a dull, leathery thud. The motor eventually started and puffs of black smoke came from the exhaust. The driver's window remained closed as the ritual of Warming Up proceeded. Aunt Craven stared straight ahead, frowning.

Then, without a backward look, she wobbled off, the

Daimler's exhaust rasping. Toby grinned at the sound. As the car turned the corner at the end of the road, there was an almighty BANG! After, the exhaust sounded worse than ever. Toby grinned more widely.

Robbie said, 'Well, she's gone,' and let his breath go.

Bets said, 'Yes, but she's coming back. In two months' time. She told me so at breakfast.'

'She told you?' said Robbie. 'She didn't bother to ask you? Or me?'

'She's not a great one for asking,' Bets said, miserably.

'The trouble is,' Toby complained to Vinny three days later, 'I actually like her rotten present. I actually like the rotten old ants. Just look at them! Stupid little gits . . .'

'Don't be rude to them,' Vinny said.

The ants never seemed to stop. They rushed after each other, over and under each other. They formed traffic jams and bottlenecks, then sorted them out by frantically constructing new motorways, bypasses, arterial roads, underpasses.

There were guard ants, soldier ants, builder/labourer ants, sanitary-squad ants and even what appeared to be loony ants. These went round in small circles, very fast, or rushed up and down the motorways for no apparent reason.

'Go-go ants,' Vinny said, pointing a fingernail at a cluster of loonies. 'Breakdance,' she said, when she found some loonies spinning about on their heads. She said, 'Do you ever get the feeling that you'd like to shake the whole thing about? But up all the roads and everything?'

'Don't!' Toby said. He looked horrified.

'Oh, so you really do like them, don't you?' Vinny said, studying his face.

'Well, yes, in a way. But you're nuts about them. You are, I know you are.'

'They're only ants,' Vinny said. Yet she stayed staring at the glass-topped box for another quarter of an hour, perhaps longer. So did Toby.

The two of them stared and stared.

Stared and stared.

Not that they'd given up Mental Magic. 'Everything we do seems to involve *staring* at something,' Vinny complained, after another attempt at making a tumbler move. 'My eyes will drop out.'

She sighed and went to look at the formicarium, bending down so that her nose almost touched the glass. 'Stare, stare, stare,' she said.

The ants scuttered and scuttled, scurried and hurried.

'You're a good little goer, aren't you?' she murmured to one ant. It had a piece of grey something or other on its back, ten times its own size. It was trying to move this enormous load from here to there, but the tides of other ants kept toppling it over, spilling the load. 'Go on, have another bash!' she encouraged the ant.

Toby joined her. 'Whoops!' he said, as yet again the ant

and its load were tipped over. 'One more time, you can do it, you're Super-Ant!' The ant fell over and its load fell off. Toby lost interest.

His mind drifted back to the glass on the table. His eyes remained on the ants, not seeing them. Why *wouldn't* the glass move? They'd tried and tried, he and Vinny, concentrating, focusing, willing, wishing. He knew every detail of the glass, he did not need to look at it. It was a cheap, moulded glass, fluted two-thirds of the way up its side. The sort of glass you get free from garages if you buy enough petrol. It had a very small chip on its rim and a slight moulding imperfection in its base, a small, shiny wart . . .

'Stupid, grotty glass!' he muttered. 'Get moving!' His mind said this while his eyes hazily took in the ever-moving panorama of the ants.

CRASH!

Startled by the noise, Toby and Vinny jerked their heads away from the formicarium, and looked behind them.

The glass was on the floor. Most of it was broken. Its base still rolled uncertainly from side to side.

'But we left it—' they both said at once.

'We left it in the middle of the table!' Toby said. 'Bang in the middle!'

'Of course we did. We always do!' Vinny said.

'Then how did it . . . ?' Toby said. Both of them were speaking in hushed whispers. Then they stopped speaking altogether, and stared at each other and the glass.

Vinny said, 'You're right. It's got to be *them*.'

They stared, silently, at the ants.

Toby said, 'Don't let's be in too much of a hurry . . . I mean, a dozen things could have made the glass move.'

'Name one,' Vinny said.

'Well . . . the wind, a draught.'

'There's no wind.'

'Well, then, perhaps you nudged the table with your backside when you were leaning over the ants.'

She leaned over the formicarium just as she had done earlier and waggled her bottom. However she waggled, there was plenty of space. 'Huh!' she said.

Toby chewed a thumbnail. Vinny began picking up the broken pieces of glass.

'So, now what?' Toby said.

'We get another glass,' Vinny said. She went to the kitchen, tipped the broken glass into the sink-tidy and came back with another cheap tumbler.

'We put the glass on the table . . . so,' she said. 'And then – *them*. The ants.'

Toby carefully placed the formicarium on the polished wood. 'Now, heads down, eyes glare, *Mindbenders!*' Vinny said.

They cupped their chins in their hands and stared at the glass, willing it to move.

25

It didn't.

'Try again,' Toby said, rubbing his eyes. Staring made his eyes itch.

They tried again. The glass did not move.

Toby gave up, leaned back and stretched his arms above his head. 'Well, that's it, as far as I'm concerned,' he said. 'Boring, boring, bor – Hey, look, Vinny! The ants!'

She looked and her mouth fell open.

The ants in the formicarium were always busy, always on the move. But now the interior of the formicarium seemed to be almost boiling. The ants were not merely scurrying: they were running, frantically. And hundreds of them were doing something Toby and Vinny had never seen before: they were hanging upside down, clinging to the glass. Because the glass was slippery, many kept falling back. Then other ants would clamber over the fallen bodies and take their turn.

Toby and Vinny watched, fascinated. Then Toby said, 'Quick, sit down, we're going to start all over again. I think I've got it!'

'Got what?'

'We've been concentrating on the wrong thing. This time, we've got to push our thoughts into the formicarium, not at the glass. We've got to get to the glass through the ants.'

'I'm not sure I know how to do that.'

''Course you do. *Look* at the ants but *think* about the glass moving.'

'That's stupid.'

'Never mind. Heads down, eyes glare, *Mindbenders!*' Vinny shrugged. 'Glass . . . *move!*' she commanded. She kept her eyes on the ants.

For a moment, she believed that the glass obeyed her will – that it did move! At any rate, in the corner of her eye, it seemed to her to twitch, to shift. 'Toby!' she whispered.

'*Concentrate!*' he hissed. She glanced at him. His eyes were wide, his mouth slightly open. He looked as if he'd seen a ghost.

He'll drive himself mad, she thought. Nevertheless, she stared at the ants and concentrated.

The glass moved. Definitely.

The glass jiggled, tottered.

The glass rattled on the table.

The glass made a small explosion – and broke.

The pieces flew. One buried itself in Vinny's forehead. A bead of blood marked the place. The bead grew. Vinny did not even notice.

Something wonderful and magical had happened. The glass had moved! They had made it move!

The first glass had broken in the ordinary, expected way – a few big pieces, lots of small pieces. This second glass seemed to have exploded. There was glass everywhere. Some fragments were so tiny that Toby went out to get some putty from the garden shed. Dabbing at the fragments with the putty seemed the best way of picking them up.

'But why?' Vinny said. 'Why did it go off like that? Did we put out too much power or something?'

'It's my voltage theory. It's got to be. The ants are supplying the extra power we needed. They're our Mindbending Multipliers!'

Vinny sat back on her heels. 'I've got a theory too.'

'Go on.'

'What were you thinking, Toby, when you were willing the glass to move?'

'I was simply thinking, "*Move*, you blankety-blank moronic glass."'

'Yes, me too. But what *exactly* were you thinking? *How* did you want the glass to move? Which direction?'

Toby said, 'Hmm!' and sat in the same position as Vinny.

'I wanted it to move towards me,' he said, slowly.

'And *I* wanted it to move towards me,' Vinny said. 'And we sat on opposite sides of the table, right?'

Toby whistled. 'So between the two of us, we *tore* the *glass in half!*' he said.

Vinny nodded. She got to her feet and threw her piece of putty into the dustpan. 'That's enough glass collecting,' she said. 'Back to work.'

'What work?'

'On the third glass,' she said. 'I'll go and get it.'

Toby studied the ants. They were behaving normally now, running up and down their little grey highways, carrying things, getting in each other's way. But when Vinny came back carrying the glass – and when she put it down on the table and said, 'There you are' – the ants went mad, as they had done before.

'Why?' Toby asked Vinny in a whisper.

'How do I know?' she said. Then – 'Why are we whispering? Ants haven't got ears.'

'But they seem to have feelings,' Toby said. 'They felt our excitement. They felt what you felt, coming in with the glass. Look at them now!'

Vinny said, 'Let's get on. Heads down, et cetera.'

'OK. But this time, we both will the same thing, right? We both will the glass to move clockwise. Agreed?'

'OK, clockwise. And it's to stop at the formicarium. When it gets there, we think, "Stop!" and that's the end of the experiment.'

'Right. We're off.'

They cupped their heads in their hands and stared. They did not have long to wait. Almost at once, the glass tilted ... turned a little ... then began to travel. It moved carefully, smoothly, not fast. It swept round the table in a clockwise curve. A small piece of broken glass must have caught in the skirt of its base, for, as it moved, it left a tiny hair-line scratch on the polished wood.

The glass reached the formicarium. Stop! Toby said in his mind. Stop! said Vinny's mind. The glass stopped.

The ants, which had till now been in a state of furious excitement, instantly quietened down.

29

Toby let out the breath he had been holding with a gasping whoosh. Vinny began saying, 'I don't believe it, I don't believe it,' over and over again.

The glass stood there, being an ordinary, cheap glass.

Twenty minutes later, Toby and Vinny had mastered all kinds of tricks with the glass. They had made it do figures-of-eight; describe circles, oblongs and squares; and, placed on its side, roll back and forth.

Without the ants, nothing happened. To make sure of this, Toby had taken the formicarium into the garden. 'I bet we can't make the glass move now,' he said. He was right. No ants, no movement.

He brought the ant colony back. The glass moved. They tried what they had decided would be the real trick, the important trick: they would *lift* the glass, make it defy the force of gravity.

The ants co-operated. They surged and scrabbled wildly as Toby and Vinny pushed their wills at the glass. The glass tried to rise. It lifted on part of its base, then another. It wanted to rise, you could see that; but it could not.

They tried again and again, but the glass would not rise. Then suddenly, without warning, Vinny started crying. Toby put an arm round her. 'What's wrong, sis?'

'I don't know. Nothing. Oh dear, oh dear . . .'

'Have I done something wrong? Is it all my fault? Go on, tell me it's all rotten old brudder's fault.' He was trying to take her back to their nursery days. He was really worried: Vinny was not the collapsing sort.

'Here, come on, hang on to me, I'm taking you up to bed.'

He put her on her bed and arranged the duvet over her. At once, she fell asleep. Her breathing was normal and her cheeks turned their normal pink even as he watched. Not a bad sister, he thought. Nice-looking. All that curling brown hair with some lighter bits in it, pointed chin, nice mouth.

He touched her forehead with the back of his finger and found it to be cool. He sighed with relief and went downstairs.

He looked at the formicarium.

The ants, he decided, were in much the same state as Vinny: flaked out. Some still ran along the roads and others clambered or tugged or dug. But all seemed to have slowed down, to be going at half-speed. All at once, Toby felt tired himself. Very tired.

He pushed the tiredness aside and continued to stare at the ants, seeing them in a new way. They seemed to swell. He could see them so clearly. Too clearly. Their gloss, their pointed heads, their brilliant eyes, their machine-like limbs always moving, always moving . . .

It suddenly occurred to him that they were a bit nasty. No, 'nasty' was too feeble. The word he wanted was something to do with super-something. Super-energetic? Super-efficient? Super-competent? Mr Rowse, who taught

31

Biology, had said that when all the world's humans had died out or killed themselves off, the ants would take over. Ants, beetles, creepy-crawlies. They would inherit the earth. It was easy to believe when you looked at them like this, with your nose close to the glass, close to those excellent little limbs that never stopped waggling and working, close to those hard, unhurtable heads and bodies, close to that endless energy, close to those mindless minds that yet obeyed a common will and purpose . . .

His tiredness overcame him. He went upstairs again, fell flat on his back on his bed and slept.

When he awoke – Robbie's key in the front door must have roused him – he thought he had dreamt something really unpleasant. He was glad to wake because the bed had become, while he slept, some sort of torture-chamber.

But dreams fade fast and Robbie was shouting, 'Didn't anyone make a cup of tea?' and Vinny was looking guilty and flustered as she sorted out her rumpled hair. Robbie liked to find Vinny in the kitchen when he came home. She cheered him up.

Downstairs, Robbie made a joke, Vinny laughed, the kettle whistled, crockery clinked.

Toby's dream faded right away.

Chapter Three

Toby had dark, V-shaped eyebrows. He thought them impressive and practised with them in front of his mirror. He could use them to make his face man-about-town, sincere, romantic – all sorts of things.

As the school was open-plan, Vinny and Toby were often close together – as they were now. She caught his eye. He raised the eyebrows to express the thought, How about trying it now?

She nodded her head very slightly. Her lips formed the word he expected: '*Mindbenders*'.

He cupped his chin in his hands. So did she. Both stared at the blackboard – stared so hard that the chalked letters and figures blurred and ran together.

In front of the blackboard stood Miss Fraser, the

teacher, who was writing on it, and an ordinary table. On the table there were some books, a blackboard eraser, a ballpoint pen belonging to the teacher and a number of chalks of various colours.

A bright mauve-pink piece of chalk took it into its head to separate itself from its fellows and roll, slowly and steadily, across the top of the table.

When it reached the edge of the table, it wobbled back and forth as if trying to make up its mind to jump; then it jumped.

It landed on the floor and broke into three pieces.

Without turning round, Miss Fraser said, tiredly, 'All right, then, who did that?'

'Not me, miss, it was him, miss, honest, miss!'

'It did it by itself, Miss Fraser!'

Pongy Peter Parker turned and hit the girl who had just spoken – Stacy Barber – with his ruler. The girl squeaked with pleasure, then screamed, 'Ooo, Miss Fraser, please stop him, he's murdering me!'

The rest of the class joined in freely and loudly. Most shouted, 'Peter pongs!' but some shouted, 'Stacy stinks!'

Just as Miss Fraser had restored order – she did it by standing with her hands on her hips and screeching, 'Quiet!' like the whistle of a steam train – the lamp bulbs began to explode, one by one.

Most of the bulbs were in white domes and bowls. These went off in a muffled sort of way, without throwing glass about. But there were also three desk lamps. The bulbs in these behaved much better. As they exploded, they spat out glass in a dramatic pattern.

The delighted class whooped, screamed, moaned, howled, stuck dividers into one another, pulled hair and even broke down in weeping fits of mock-terror.

The only quiet children were Toby and Vinny. Vinny quietly said a word to her brother: 'Brill!' was the word.

'Super-colossal!' he replied.

A minute later, everyone was out in the playground because of the risk of getting cut by glass. Break wasn't due for twenty minutes, so the mood was a happy one. 'Great, isn't it?' Pongy Peter Parker grinned.

'Oh,' Toby said, with massive modesty, 'it was nothing really. But I'm glad you're pleased.' He wriggled his eyebrows in his special modest way. 'Don't bother to thank me,' he said.

'What're you talking about?' Pongy asked. 'What have you got to do with the lights?'

'I made them blow up, that's all,' Toby said.

Pongy Peter gave a scornful 'Guhrr!' and walked off.

Vinny joined her brother. 'You shouldn't have said that, moron,' she told Toby.

'He didn't believe me. People never believe the truth. We're as safe as houses.'

'All the same . . .' Vinny said, uneasily. Then – 'Besides, you didn't blow up the lights. Not just *you*. We *both* did it.'

'Yes, well, sorry,' Toby said. 'You're right, it takes

both of us. Not that it matters. What really matters
is—'

'The ants!' Vinny said, quietly but intensely.

Blowing light bulbs was already as easy as pie. Or as easy
as rolling a piece of chalk. It had taken them only a week
or so to master tricks like that.

At first, the formicarium had to be there. They had
to look at the ants, have the ants right in front of them,
direct their thoughts through them to 'step up the voltage'.
But as time passed, everything became both simpler and
stronger. Simpler, because they could distance themselves
from their medium, their stepper-up of 'voltage', their
Mindbending Multipliers: the ants. Stronger, because
their powers seemed to grow stronger every day.

Once, moving a glass had drained them and driven the
ants to a sort of frenzy. Now, their minds could send a
glass spinning like a top across the table. They could send
a mental dart through the envelope of a light bulb and
watch it implode. All without ants.

School was a riot. First, all the lights went off and
every-one whistled or went, 'Ooooo!'

'Please, teacher, I'm so *frightened!*' squeaked Boffer
Baker, the biggest and toughest boy in the school. He
made a great thing of trying to hide under Sally Forester's
desk. When he squeezed her legs, she squealed.

Everyone was shouting, 'There're bogeymen!'

'Ooo, it's all dark, I'm scared!'

'Mummy, hold me tight!'

The teacher didn't have a chance.

At last Toby raised an eyebrow at Vinny – and the lights came on and stayed on. 'Let's burst some bulbs, just to finish off,' she said. He shook his head. Later, she said, 'You're right. It's not real fun when they don't know it's us who're doing it.'

'Marvellous old us,' Toby said. 'Soon, we'll show our hands – reveal all. Meantime, extra rations for the ants.'

When they got home, they gave the ants an extra helping of what seemed to be their favourite food: currants.

Apparently, the ants would eat anything. Crumbs, leaves, dead insects, scraps of leftovers – everything went down the tube sticking out of the side of the formicarium and disappeared. But currants were the thing, you could see them cluster round a currant.

That evening, the formicarium received three whole currants.

A day or so later at school, Vinny and Toby made the computers go mad.

They intended it to be an impressive demonstration, and it was. For whatever you keyed in to the school computers, you always got the same printout . . .

TV FOR QUEEN

or, TV FOR KING
or, TV RULE, OK?

It delighted the pupils and drove the teachers mad.

'Let me have a go, sir!'

'No, stand back, you stupid boy, *I'll* do it.' The teacher did it and the screen said:

TV RULE, OK?

'It's not even *grammatical*,' complained Mrs Loveday, Head of English. 'It should be "TV *RULES*, OK?" with an *s*.'

'Do you think so?' Toby and Vinny said, their faces innocent and interested.

Inwardly, they hugged themselves, because they alone knew what the mad messages meant. 'TV' stood for 'Toby and Vinny'. So the grammar was right.

In the playground a ring of children formed round them. '*Did* you do it? *How* did you do it?'

'Mental Magic,' Toby said, smiling knowingly and mockingly.

'Garn! There's no such thing!'

'Of course not,' Toby agreed. 'There's no such thing, is there, Vinny?'

'It *sounds* impossible,' she said.

Ginger Bailey, a big boy, said, 'Do something magic *now* in front of us all, or you'll get thumped.'

'I don't think you should threaten us,' Vinny said sweetly.

'You want this in your hooter?' Ginger said, showing her a large red fist.

'I've got a fist of my own, thank you,' Vinny said, politely. 'And mine's *clean*.'

Ginger thrust his face at her and said, 'You want to watch it, you two!'

'Watch it?' Toby said. He gave Vinny a split-second sideways glance. 'Watch it? he repeated. She gave the slightest of nods.

Ginger's prized possession was his wristwatch – an electronic-digital-stopwatch-calculator-alarm thing about the size of a mince pie. 'How is your watch?' Vinny asked Ginger.

'Never mind my watch,' Ginger said. 'Just you get on with some magic.'

'Oh, but we have,' Vinny said.

'Try the stopwatch,' Toby suggested.

Ginger growled, pressed a button on the watch – and gaped. 'It's going *backwards!*' he said, in a sort of howl. Everyone wanted to look. '37, 36, 35, 34, 33, 32,' the watch went.

'Here, I'll smash your face in!' Ginger said. But at that moment the watch went beep and someone started laughing. Ginger slunk away, scarlet and baffled.

Everyone else stared at Vinny and Toby, goggleeyed. 'Go on, tell us, how do you do it?' they asked. But Vinny's only answer was to look innocent; and Toby's only reply was to waggle his eyebrows significantly.

'How do we do it?' Toby mused, when he and Vinny were home.

'Well, it's obvious,' Vinny said. 'We concentrate and the formicarium steps up our "voltage" and there you are. What I want to know is, what do we do next?'

'Get rich,' Toby said. 'Become showbiz sensations. Make pots of money. Appear on TV and everything.'

'Oh, yes!' Vinny said. 'But first we want to work out a proper act. I mean, so far all we do is what looks like conjuring. We know it's more than that, but people watching wouldn't know. I wonder . . . I wonder if we could magick *living* things . . . ?'

Which is how Bloggs's Mystical Mouse came into being.

'If we can do a mouse,' Toby said, 'perhaps we could do a moose! That would stun everyone! Think of the money we'd get if we could magick really big animals!'

'You're always thinking about money,' Vinny said.

'Aren't you?'

'Of course! There're so many things I want!'

'When we're the Mindbending Mites with the Marvellous Minds, stars of stage, screen and TV, we'll be able to afford anything we want!' Toby said. 'Video camera, ten-speed lightweight bike—'

'Yes, I know all that,' Vinny interrupted. 'But how do we start? I mean, we're minors, we can't be stars of this and that because we're too young. We've got to have an adult behind us, fixing things.'

Toby said, 'Well, there's Mum and Dad.'

'You're joking, of course,' Vinny said. 'All they think of is getting us ready for our exams. And they're not exactly showbiz folk, are they?'

Toby sighed. 'Well, no. So where do we start? Who do we talk to?'

In the end, they decided to start with Greg Stewkeley.

Greg inspired confidence. Inspiring confidence was vital to his career.

He owned a firm on the nearby trading estate called Lektronic Enterprises. It supplied business systems, computers and specialist electronic devices. He also owned a current-model Jaguar with Connolly leather seats. When you came too close to this car, it said, in plain words, 'No closer, friend. Keep your distance. Thank you.' One of Greg's electronic gadgets did the voice. As Greg also owned an Alsatian called Garth, and as Garth had strong white teeth, nobody argued with the electronic voice.

Greg was in his early thirties. He had a big, round, highly coloured face and warm brown eyes. His handshake was warm too. He shook hands a lot. With your hand safely contained in both of his and those sincere eyes on yours, you felt, Greg will get it done. Greg will see it through. Greg himself liked to say, 'No sweat! Just leave it to old Greg!' Money to rebuild the cricket pavilion? Posters for a jumble sale? No sweat.

'He's a phoney,' Vinny said, when Toby first suggested taking their secret to Greg.

'Maybe he is,' Toby said. 'But he gets things moving. You can't deny it.'

Vinny couldn't deny it, so they took Greg into their confidence.

His office was on the top floor of the Lektronic building. Chrome, smoked glass, soft leather and potted plants were everywhere. Greg's long-legged secretary brought them coffee and little honey cakes from Germany. 'Only for my very special visitors,' Greg beamed at them. He threw a cake high into the air and caught it in his mouth. Toby clapped his hands, but Vinny said, 'We know better tricks than that, Mr Stewkeley.'

'Ho-kay, hokey-kokey, tell me all about it!' Greg said, settling back in his big leather-and-chrome swivelling chair.

They told him.

When they'd finished, Greg threw another honey cake, caught it in his mouth and said, pleasantly, 'I don't believe you.'

Vinny said, 'You want us to show you?'

'But definitely,' Greg said. He started doing exercises in and on his armchair. 'Amaze me,' he said.

Within minutes, Greg had stopped doing exercises. He

had stopped doing anything, in fact, except stare as the tumbler on his desk slid slowly across the polished surface to end up in his hand ... as his secretary's electronic typewriter endlessly typed MENTAL MAGIC RULES OK MENTAL MAGIC RULES OK.

'Holy bedsocks!' he said at last, in a voice that shook. He could say nothing more for some time. He could only shake hands repeatedly with Vinny and Toby and say the word, 'Fantastic!' in a sort of gasp.

'So you'll help us get rich and famous and all that?' Toby said. He expected the long-legged secretary to be summoned and to start typing contracts and agreements and so on right away.

But all Greg would say was, 'Give me *time*. Let me *think*.'

Toby and Vinny went away with nothing settled. 'But we certainly impressed him,' Vinny said. 'I mean, he's bound to want to get in on the act. Manage us, or whatever.'

'No sweat!' Toby grinned.

When Toby and Vinny had gone and Greg was alone in his office, his face changed. It became colder and older.

'It had to happen some time,' he muttered to himself. '*Someone, somewhere* had to find the secret ...'

He went to the window and stared down at Garth, guarding his Jaguar. 'I mean,' he said to himself, 'it's only logical. A couple of centuries of technological advances ... engineering, electrical, scientific, the microchip ... A few centuries of *that* – then someone comes along and short-circuits the whole thing. Someone finds another route, another way, another method of doing things. A no-sweat, no-switches way. And that's the end of me and my business.'

Greg pressed a button and his secretary whisked in, nylons a-twinkle. 'Yes, Mr Stewkeley?'

'Take a letter.'

'Yes, Mr Stewkeley.'

'Dear Vinny and Toby – that's the two kids who just left. Got their address?'

'Yes, Mr Stewkeley.'

He dictated the letter. Later, she brought it to him to sign. The letter read:

Dear Vinny and Toby,

I have now had time to think over the matter we discussed this afternoon.

You want my advice. Here it is.

Don't do anything. Don't say anything.

Just leave things to Greg.

Remember, not a word to anyone.

In touch very soon.

All the best.

Yours sincerely,
Greg

'There you are,' Toby said next day, when the letter arrived. 'That's not a phoney letter, is it? Well, is it?'

'No,' Vinny admitted. 'But it doesn't tell us anything.'

'Oh yes, it does. It tells us to keep our big mouths shut and not go round showing off our Mindbending.'

'I suppose so,' Vinny said. She was not really listening to her brother. She was thinking of the formicarium.

She had had an accident with the formicarium. She had dropped it.

It was a very small accident and not important, surely? All that had happened was – *bump*, formicarium upside-down on carpet, clumsy me, but no harm done, glass not even cracked, thank goodness, ants a bit shaken up, can't blame them – but what's this?

The binding stuff holding the glass to the box had become unstuck! But only in this corner. Get that transparent glue, stick the binding tape down.

She found the glue, made an invisible mend and congratulated herself on her neatness.

Then, out of the corner of her eye, she saw something move.

An ant. No, several ants! She could not tell just how many, the pile of the carpet hid them.

So, some of the ants had got free.

Did it matter? No. Was she sorry for the poor, homeless escapers? No. Ants knew how to take care of themselves. Ants didn't care.

All the same, she studied the formicarium with great attention when she put it back where it belonged, on the table. They really were very busy. Not just because of being dropped: they were busy in a particular way, a new way. There was a concentrated mass of them in one corner – a wriggling, seething cluster of furiously busy little bodies.

Of course! A Queen!

The ants had created a Queen, that was it. She knew all about it from the ant books. There was a Queen – probably more than one. She would, with the help of the workers, produce cocoons containing larvae – baby ants. Eggs, larvae, pupae. Then proper baby ants. The workers would clean and feed the brood constantly. She and Toby would see the whole process. Terrific!

When Toby came in, Vinny fluttered her eyelashes at him and said, coyly, 'I think I am going to be a mother!'

'Ha, ha,' he said, unamused. 'Who's the father?'

'You,' she said.

'Ha, *ha*,' he said.

But when she showed him the formicarium, he was as thrilled as she was.

By that time, the ants that had escaped were any-where at all – perhaps under floorboards, perhaps mak-ing their way through the brickwork of the house to the great outdoors. Vinny knew that wherever they were, they would soon make themselves at home. So she did not bother to mention the Great Escape to Toby.

Chapter Four

Things happened fast to Vinny and Toby.

There was a letter from Aunt Craven. Soon she would return, for a long stay.

The formicarium was going crazy about the new brood.

School said Toby's homework wasn't good enough and if he wanted to pass his exams, he'd better get his head down as of now.

And Greg Stewkeley telephoned. 'Meet me Saturday – 12.45 by the 'phone box outside the trading estate, right?' he said. 'But not a word to anyone. You be there, I'll pick you both up in the Jaguar, you know my Jaguar? Good. And don't say a dicky-bird. Roger, wilco and out.'

* * *

Saturday, 12.45. The Jaguar came alongside them like a liner docking and eased to a halt. 'In you get,' Greg said. 'That's right, in the back. Relax, lean back, enjoy yourselves.'

The Jaguar made a slight surging noise. Cushioned leather pushed into Toby's and Vinny's backs.

'Super car,' Toby said. Greg beamed over his shoulder. 'Do a hundred and thirty, no sweat,' he said.

Vinny was silent and embarrassed. She did not quite know why. Perhaps it was the presence of the chauffeur, the man in the driver's seat? But he couldn't be a chauffeur. His dark suit was too well cut, his collar too white, cufflinks too gold-and-pearly.

Greg saw her fascination. He said, 'Ooops, beg pardons, haven't introduced you! Vinny, Toby – meet Barry. Barry da Silva, the money man. Very ongoing personage money-wise, our Barry.'

For the first time, Barry turned to face Vinny and Toby. 'Nice to meet you,' he said, tonelessly. His shadowed eyes were dark and flat. 'You're the ones with the mental powers, is that right? Mental powers. Very interesting proposition.'

Vinny did not like his eyes. She turned to Greg and said, 'Why meet here, in the car? Why not in your office?'

Greg beamed and said, 'Business very confidential. Confidential, very. Even walls have ears, did you know that? Oh yes, they do. We want to keep things top-secret, agreed? Hey, Barry, how about stopping here?'

Barry slid the car into a dead-end lane flanked with tall grasses and cow-parsley. He switched off the engine. Birds quarrelled in the hedges. 'Now we'll talk business,' Greg said.

Barry swivelled round in his seat. 'This Mental Magic stuff,' he said. 'You really can do it?'

'Of course we can!' Vinny said, speaking too loudly. She was wondering if Barry da Silva's face could be made of plastic, the best plastic, with pores and hairs added one by one.

'We can do it, all right,' Toby said. His own voice sounded hollow to him.

'Good, fine,' Barry said. 'Give us a demo, here and now.'

Toby whispered to Vinny. She nodded. Toby said, 'Just switch on the ignition so that all the electrical things can work.'

Barry nodded and turned the ignition key. Little lights lit and neat needles flicked on the dashboard.

'That light in the mirror,' Toby announced. The light came on, went off, came on again – then blazed so brilliantly that the bulb gave a small pop and burned out.

'Indicators!' said Vinny. The green arrows on the dashboard flickered left, right, left, right, left-right-left,

'Instruments,' Toby said. All the needles on all the dials began dancing. They went so fast that they made tiny chittering noises.

'Enough, *enough!*' said Barry da Silva.

There was a long silence until Toby said, 'Well?' He expected someone to say, 'Fantastic!' or 'Marvellous!' But the two men simply sat and stared at nothing.

At last Barry said to Greg, 'Make them the offer.'

Toby and Vinny exchanged glances, baffled.

'Ah, the offer,' Greg said. He gave a big smile. 'This you will like!' he said. 'It's a generous offer. Really generous, because you're great kids, both of you. And nice with it. Really nice.'

Toby and Vinny kept quiet.

'Now, a couple of nice kids like you wouldn't want to cause anyone trouble, would you?' Greg continued. 'Especially your old pal Greg?'

Vinny said, 'We're not interested in causing trouble, all we're interested in is doing an *act* . . . amazing people, being stars and everything—'

'And money,' Toby said. 'We want to make lots of money and be rich and famous.'

'Money,' Barry said, flatly. 'Money's no problem. Money you want, money you'll get.'

'Money's what we're offering,' Greg said. 'Take a look!' He pulled out his wallet. It was black with gold edges. It bulged. He pulled out a roll of notes and peeled off fivers, one at a time. He beamed and sweated as he slapped the notes one on top of another on the curve of his seat's backrest. The pile toppled and notes fell on the carpeted floor.

'Yours, all yours,' he beamed. 'A hundred pounds! In lovely Bank of England fivers! Go on – take 'em!'

'But what's the money *for*?' Vinny said.

'What do we have to *do*?' said Toby.

'It's money for nothing!' Greg said. 'Yours for doing nothing!'

'*Absolutely* nothing,' Barry da Silva said. 'You take our point?'

Vinny shook her head vigorously. 'No,' she began. 'We want—'

'You want more?' Barry said. 'Smart kids. Tell you what: you take Mr Stewkeley's hundred and I'll add another fifty of my own. Here you are – five tenners.'

'But—' Toby said.

'A hundred and fifty pounds, grab it while the offer holds,' said Barry. He pulled back a white cuff and looked at his gold wristwatch. 'We've got a lot of business on our hands this afternoon,' he said.

Greg looked solemn, and said, 'Yep. Time flies. Let's settle up and move on.' He pushed a handful of notes on to Vinny's lap.

Vinny tried to refuse the money. Toby said, 'Look, we can't take money for nothing.'

Greg smiled, winked and said, 'Of course you can. You do *nothing*, right? Absolutely *nothing*. That's the deal.'

'Nothing, now or ever,' Barry said. He too began thrusting notes at Vinny.

Suddenly she had had enough. On one side of her was

the bobbing pink balloon of Greg's face; on the other, the sallow, serpent face of the plastic man. 'I want to go home,' she said, shakily. She opened the door and began scrambling out, half expecting to be grabbed and held. But Toby was getting out too, it would be all right, they'd get away . . .

Even as she cleared the car and felt rough grass against her ankles, she thought, Get away from *what*?

Then they were half walking, half running home.

They slowed down when it was obvious that the Jaguar was not pursuing them. Toby said, 'You didn't half get in a panic! Leaping out of the car and everything!'

Vinny said, 'I couldn't stand it in there any more. I couldn't stand it and I couldn't understand it either. I mean, what were they on about? All that talk of money for nothing?'

'Oh, that's obvious,' Toby said loftily. 'I worked that one out yonks ago.'

'Well, I haven't, so explain it to me.'

'Look: we can make things work with our minds, right? By Mindbending. We can switch things on and off and make a fool of a computer and all that . . .'

'I don't care about that part,' Vinny said. 'All I care about is being stars, and rich and famous.'

'Yes, but that's not how Greg sees it! I mean, just think. His business, his whole life, is switches and circuits and chips, microelectronics . . . Then we come along, and all the things he does for a living we do for a giggle!'

'You mean, we're a threat to him?' Vinny said.

'Worse than a threat, we're deadly poison!'

'And that's why that Barry da Silva man' – she shuddered – 'kept saying the money's for doing nothing?'

'Of course. They were trying to pay us to go away. To shut up, do nothing, un-invent ourselves, forget all about Mindbending.'

Vinny said, 'But that's awful! It means he's our enemy! A crook!'

'Not necessarily. It just means he's frightened of us. He's not a baddie or a crook or anything. He's just scared stiff. I don't blame him. We could make him go broke.'

'Then why didn't he offer us more money? Lots more?'

'Offering too much would show us he was on to us. A huge offer would make us suspicious.'

'I don't know . . .' Vinny said. 'I suppose he's not really bad.'

'Not bad. Just businesslike,' Toby said.

They turned the last corner. Their home was in view. Parked outside it was a large, solemn car. Aunt Craven's Daimler.

'Hell's bells, she's back!' Toby said.

She was back all right: and with Aunt Craven's arrival everything went back to abnormal. Bets's fixed, welcoming smile was so wide that you could see her molars.

Aunt Craven herself seemed in her usual form. 'Hallo, you two horrors!' she greeted Vinny and Toby. 'What's this I hear about the formicarium? The ants are actually still alive and kicking? Wonders will never cease! Never thought you'd have the gumption to look after them!'

She began issuing orders. Robbie wouldn't mind taking a rag to the Daimler's distributor, would he? Give it a bit of a clean-up? Starting had been a bit umpty of late. And Bets had got in some fennel tea, hadn't she? Can't stand your Indian or Ceylon, rots the gut, herbal teas are the thing . . .

Toby and Vinny tried to escape, but the Aunt grappled them to her. 'Tell me about the ants!' she commanded.

'Well,' Vinny said, 'the Queen's laying babies and everything.'

'Preggers, eh?' laughed Aunt Craven. She had to be shown the formicarium. She insisted on knowing best about how to feed the Queen, the right temperature and place for the formicarium – everything. Yet, as she bossed the children about, a soft gleam appeared in her eyes. 'She's going all maternal,' Vinny whispered to Toby. 'Mother love!'

Toby muttered, 'Mother love? *Her?*'

'Well,' Aunt Craven said at last, 'I suppose you've done the best you can. Everything *looks* in order.'

'Oh, the ants are all right,' Toby said. 'And you're all right, are you, Aunt Craven?'

She glared and replied, 'All right for what?'

'All right for cigarettes,' Toby said, innocently.

Aunt Craven turned a funny colour, began to speak, couldn't, and stamped out. Toby grinned.

Vinny looked thoughtful. 'I think we'd better lay off the Aunt-baiting for a while,' she said.

Toby said, 'Why?'

'Well, I think we're getting at her too much. She looks a bit, I don't know, shattered.'

'Aunt Craven shattered? She's unshatterable!' Toby said. He shrugged and said, 'Let's have a look at our little chums, then.'

They bent over the formicarium.

The Queen saw two enormous white blobs descend over the Queendom. The Queen could not put a name to the blobs, which were, of course, the faces of Vinny and Toby. But she could, now, see some meaning behind the familiar apparitions. She could even feel a sort of excitement when they appeared.

She needed excitement, for her life was now empty. So was her body. She had laid all her eggs. Now her servants took over. They nursed and nurtured her innumerable children. The Queen had time to think. And this Queen, uniquely, *could* think.

Thoughts flooded her mind . . .

I am the great and glorious Queen of Queens, she thought, mistress of an empire, mother of countless warriors. I am great and glorious and powerful . . .

She was right. Ants are powerful. They always have been, always will be. Great builders, they can tunnel, fortify, conceive elaborate towns and cities. Great warriors, they can defend themselves singly or attack in the mass, using flesh-tearing mandibles and paralysing chemical weapons.

Above all, they communicate. The Queen commands; and her messages are passed on, chemically and in other ways, from cleaner to warrior, from explorer to builder . . . Or even telepathically, from mind to mind.

I am great, the Queen thought, but I can see and understand that I am small. Those great living blobs out there – they are alive, like me. And they can communicate. But they are enormous. So their physical powers, their tools and toys, must be enormous too . . .

So what is it I want? I know! I want what they have got – the things they have taught me about, the things that have entered my mind from their minds . . .

They have so much! They are so huge, so powerful! And they have so much equipment, so many things that could be weapons.

I want them. When I have them, I will conquer and rule their larger world.

But how can I get them? My kingdom is so small, and there seems to be no way out of it. Around me there are walls I cannot penetrate. Beneath me is a floor that even the sharpest jaws cannot bite through. Above me there is blackness (she was thinking of the black cloth that usually covered the formicarium); or a shiny nothing, slippery and impermeable (she was thinking of the glass cover); or the great white blobs.

So there is no escape from this world. But still I must find a way to rule that greater world outside. How? How?

The answer came to her shortly after her thoughts were interrupted by a call from outside: a call that entered her mind much as a telephone call enters your house. There is a signal, you obey it, you receive a communication . . .

The call was from the new Daughter Queen, mistress of the escaped ants. The New Queen's apartments had been established some seventy metres from the house among the roots of an old, split tree. The earth was easy to work there and rotten bark harboured living food.

'It's me, Your Majesty!' said the New Queen, slightly flustered. 'Your Daughter Queen . . .'

'Indeed. Well, what do you want?'

'Only to pay my respects, Your Majesty, and tell you about my eggs. Yes, I'm full of eggs! I get so tired. But soon, of course—'

'What do you *want?*'

'I was just wondering if my colony – and all the lovely new babies to come – could be of service to you in any way. Even, perhaps, an alliance—'

'An *alliance?* Between you and *me?* Ha!'

'I was only thinking—'

The 'line' went dead. Yet, as she cut off, the Old Queen suddenly saw the answer she needed. She reopened the 'line'.

'There is, after all,' the Old Queen said, 'a small service you can perform for me.'

'Oh, Your Majesty, of course! Anything at all!'

'You are soon to give birth, you say?'

'Well, quite soon, Your Majesty, I think.'

'I myself,' said the Old Queen, 'have long ago completed my cycle. My eggs are all laid, capped and progressing very nicely.'

'I am sure they are, Your Majesty.'

'Do not interrupt. Splendid as the Royal brood is, I have recently formulated in my mind a requirement involving children of superior warrior capability.'

'Could you put it more simply, Your Majesty?'

'You are to breed big ants.'

'Oh, I *see*, Your Majesty. Big ants. Certainly, Your Majesty. But . . . but just *how*, Your Majesty?'

'I will send a messenger with instructions and dietary formulae. Special foods. You will follow these instructions exactly. Meanwhile, you will command your workers to enlarge the nest.'

'By how much, Your Majesty?'

'By an enormous amount. For an enormous brood chamber to accommodate enormous ants.'

'Yes, Your Majesty.'

'You may commence operations without delay. That means, immediately.'

'Yes, Your Majesty.'

The very next day, Aunt Craven ran out of cigarettes. Her Daimler was misbehaving and making funny noises; this meant that she had to swallow her pride and ask Toby to bike to the village to get more.

'Oh, of *course* I'll go, Aunt Craven!' Toby said, his voice all holy and sympathetic. 'You must have your ciggies!'

'That dreadful *craving!*' Vinny echoed. 'How terrible for you!'

The next day, Toby had to go to the village again because Aunt Craven wanted oat flakes.

He got his bike out and had to pump the front tyre. With every stroke of the pump, he let fly a different swear word. He found he knew only eleven and this made him angrier than ever.

He pedalled along, thinking of Aunt Craven and the various tortures that would suit her best. But soon the sound and feeling of his bike put him in a mellower mood, and he thought seriously about his aunt. Why was she so bossy and booming? Why did she feel it necessary to have people run errands for her? Why did she have to dominate everyone?

Inferiority complex! his mind answered. But no, that was too cheap and easy an answer. And anyhow, Aunt Craven wasn't inferior. She was the tough one of the whole family, the successful one, the one who'd made it.

He had just reached a decision – that Aunt Craven was a mix-up, a tough nut with a well hidden soft centre – when a big Jaguar brought him back to reality by squeezing him into the curb. Its driver, Greg Stewkeley, beamed and waved at him from the driver's seat.

'A word in your ear, young sir!' Greg said, cheerily. Toby had to get off his bike and listen.

'About our little business meeting the other day,' Greg began. Toby kept his face blank and cold. 'Bit of a frost, wasn't it?' Greg said. 'Got off on the wrong foot. All my fault, bringing Barry along. Little sister did not like him, did she? Not one bit. Not her type. Confidentially, he's not always my type either, but he knows about money, he really does.'

'Money!' Toby said. 'We weren't after your money. When you both started pushing money at us—'

'Just what I mean!' Greg said. 'Got us off on the wrong foot, all those fivers. Because what you're interested in is getting an act together, right? 'Course you are. Money isn't top priority, OK?'

'Well, it doesn't matter now,' Toby began.

'Ah, but it does matter! It matters to me! You see, I'm still interested, very interested, in this Mindbender proposition. You two are great, you know that? And I still want to help you any way I can. I kid you not. Now, suppose we started all over again, just the three of us? I could fix a meeting in my office any time, any day, no sweat. Then we could—'

Toby said, 'We shouldn't have come to you in the first place. Look, I've got to get to the shops before they close.' He threw his leg over his bike, determined to get away.

Greg had to lean out of his window. 'Listen, listen!' he said, keeping the smile on his face. 'All I want you to know is this. You're on to something big, you two! Bigger than you understand.'

'I'll keep in touch,' Toby said. He began to pedal away. Greg's voice followed him. 'You need help, you call me any time!' he shouted. 'I mean it!'

Toby waved his hand without looking back and pedalled on.

The Jaguar came past, tucking down its rear end as it accelerated. 'Any time at all, no sweat!' Greg shouted above the hissing surge of the car.

Chapter Five

Bloggs the cat was elderly, respectable and habit-bound. He began his day with a breakfast of the smelliest tinned fish food available. He turned his nose up at un-smelly food. Breakfast over, he went to Vinny's bed and cleaned himself, leaving a circle of black hairs around him for Vinny to complain about later.

Around teatime, when Toby and Vinny came back from school, he gulped down more horrible food and leaped on Vinny's shoulder, breathing fishy smells at her. She complained about this too.

In the evening, he watched TV with the family: not with much interest, as most programmes sent him to sleep. When something really exciting came on the screen, Bloggs always demanded to be let out for the night. If it was cold or raining, he stood half in and half out of the door, twitching. Everyone complained about this habit, yet none of them could find it in their hearts to kick his furry bottom, because Bloggs gave everyone pleasure. He sat on laps, purred loudly, presented you with dead mice and did his best to join in ball games on the lawn. He was Family.

That morning – perhaps two or three weeks after the two Queens' conversation – Vinny and Toby were gobbling their breakfasts and telling each other to hurry or they'd be late for school.

Vinny said, 'Where's Bloggs?'

Toby said, 'Never mind him, finish your toast.'

Vinny said, 'But where *is* he? He's always in by now. I'm worried.'

She went to the back door for the third time. She opened it, and Bloggs more or less fell into the kitchen, sprawling over her shoes and wetting them with blood.

He was in an awful state. He was bleeding from his ear, forehead, shoulder and one hind leg.

Vinny began crying, almost screaming. Toby said, 'Get out of the *way*, let me *look* at him!' and examined Bloggs's injuries, secretly terrified by what he saw. Bets, hearing Vinny, rushed in. Bloggs was put on a cushion. He behaved nobly. He let Toby and Bets explore his injuries. He even gave his usual greeting chirrup.

Bets said, 'You two get off to school. I'll see to this.'

They went, Vinny in floods of tears all the way.

Then Aunt Craven marched into the kitchen. 'What's all the fuss!' she demanded, her chin up and her shoulders square. Bets was too busy with Bloggs to answer, so Aunt Craven had to bend over the thing on the cushion and see for herself.

She jerked upright – and made a funny noise: a noise so strange that Bets forgot Bloggs for a moment.

Bets saw that Aunt Craven's face had gone a deadly white and that she was trembling, violently. 'The blood!' Aunt Craven said. 'Oh, the blood! Oh, poor thing, it's bleeding . . .'

Then, astoundingly, she fainted.

She came to quickly and completely. 'So stupid, what a fool, you must think me a complete idiot!' she barked.

'No, I don't.'

'I can't bear to see an animal suffer. And the blood—'

'I understand, honestly. Look, Craven, we've got to get Bloggs to the vet. Immediately. I'll have to hold Bloggs, so I can't drive. Get your car started. Hurry.'

Aunt Craven nodded – she was still very white – and ran to her car. She put the key in. The engine fired. It ran lumpily, because the choke was out – then, suddenly, began making an appalling noise, a clattering, thumping death-rattle. Aunt Craven switched off the engine, got out and inspected her car.

Underneath the bonnet, a thick, dark shining pool of oil spread, creeping into and then along the gutter.

Now her face was whiter than ever.

Bets had to drive to the vet in her Mini, with Bloggs in her lap and her sister beside her, crying. Crying! Craven crying!

The vet said, 'Poor old thing, he's been attacked. No, I don't know by what. Not by a human, I don't think . . . He's been *torn at* by something. A fox? No, nor a dog. It's as if he's been run over by a farm machine, something with hooks under it. Oh, I apologize, I didn't mean to upset you . . .

'Oh yes, he'll be fine. Cats are about the toughest creatures going, you'd be amazed. Antibiotics, stitches – that's right, you go outside while I get to work on him. Won't be long. Then get him home and make a fuss of him. He'll see to his own recovery. No, I promise you, he will be all right, he really will.'

Bloggs stayed quiet even when the needle went in. 'Good old fellow, aren't you?' the vet said. Bloggs blinked and politely purred.

Back home, Bets settled Bloggs in the warmest part of the kitchen. He purred approvingly. He even tried to eat some food. Eventually he went to sleep.

Aunt Craven, still shaking, said, 'You must think me a fool. Behaving so badly, being so useless.'

Bets said, 'Nonsense. I'll just 'phone the school so that someone can tell the kids Bloggs is all right.'

She made the call. When she came back, Aunt Craven

had her head in her hands. Tears dripped from the fingers.

Bets was astonished. 'Craven, don't! Everything's all right, really it is! Come on, now!'

Aunt Craven said, 'All that blood! Poor old cat . . .'

'But it's over, he's OK. You heard the vet.'

'Your poor pet cat, my poor pet car,' Aunt Craven said, indistinctly. 'Everything piling up . . . people gunning for me at work . . . the car will cost a fortune.'

'But, Craven, surely you can afford to have the car mended?'

'Oh yes, oh yes, that's right!' Aunt Craven burst out. 'Craven will cope! Craven's so blasted rich and successful, isn't she? Financial journalists earn pots of money, don't they? Ha *ha*, in a pig's eye they do! If they close down my newspaper – which they threaten to do – how does rich, successful Craven cope then? As if you cared!'

'But, Craven . . . !' Bets started. Before she could say more, Aunt Craven said, 'Oh, don't take any notice of me. I'm behaving like a complete moron. And taking it out on you. Well, I would, wouldn't I? I've always been so jealous of you!'

For the second time, Bets was astounded.

'*Jealous*? Of me? But that's mad! You're the successful one, you always were, even at school! Prizes and cups and scholarships and everything!'

'But you were the pretty one, the real, proper *girl*,' Aunt Craven said, bitterly. 'Dad adored you. So I had to concentrate on being good at things. Which I was, and look where it's got me. Jealous idiot, jealous, jealous.'

She sat upright, tightened her mouth and said, 'Well, there you are. All over. And quite enough too! Can I pinch some tissues? I must look an absolute *joke*. Well, I am a sort of joke, really, aren't I? Bossing people about, smoking forty a day, going in for old Daimlers and funny religions and all that. I've worked all my life to become a mixed-up idiot and look at me now!'

Bets said, 'Well, you are an idiot. There you are, the big-wheel journalist, radio and telly appearances and all that; and here's me, just another mum; and *you* envy *me!*'

They stared at each other uncertainly. Then both began giggling. Bets said, 'Go on, sis, giss a kiss!'

Before, their kisses had been like soldiers' salutes: the rules say 'Do it', so you do it. This kiss was quite different.

Vinny and Toby went straight to Bloggs when they got home from school. Toby tried to look gruff and uncaring. Vinny did not bother to conceal her feelings. She even kissed the bandaged bits. Bloggs let her do whatever she wanted and occasionally blinked or put his front paw on her nose, like a bishop blessing someone.

'I'm so *relieved*, I'm so *glad*,' Vinny gushed. Then she said, 'Can I go to bed for an hour before dinner, Mum? I'm flaked out. I've been so worried about Bloggs.'

'Yes, of course. Take a mug of tea with you.'

Vinny went upstairs. She lay down, drank half her tea and instantly fell asleep.

Vinny dreamed.

First, she dreamed of Bloggs. He was having some sort of fit (she had seen a cat having fits) and his eyes had changed colour, they had gone white. He writhed and twisted and tried to bite himself, glaring at her with white, sightless eyes.

The dream was so horrible that it jerked her awake. To reassure herself, she sat up in bed and said, aloud, 'Bloggs is all right. It was only a stupid dream. Finish your tea.' The tea was slightly warm, so she could not have been dreaming long.

She went back to sleep and dreamed again.

This time, it was the formicarium. All the ants were doing somersaults and tricks. They seemed very big and clear, she could see everything they did perfectly. Some ants were doing their tricks in chorus, all at the same time, and the Queen's voice was right in her ear doing a commentary. The Queen sounded like the gymnast lady on TV. '*A lovely exercise,*' the voice said, '*such perfect unison. I think 9.7 at* least. *And such a lovely feeling for the music.*'

Vinny thought, Stupid woman, I wish she'd shut up, I can't hear the music at all. However hard she listened, there was no music. There *ought* to be music, this sort of display needed music.

Then she heard it. It was rotten music, not even in time with the ants. TAP, TAP-TAP, TAP . . . TAP, went the music. No tune at all, just an out-of-time tapping and scraping. Vinny adjusted the formicarium's brightness and contrast – this formicarium had TV controls – but it made no difference. Adjusting the volume simply made the Queen's voice louder: '*A very big impression*,' the voice said. '*Very big indeed*.'

'Big, really big, no sweat!' echoed the voice of Greg Stewkeley. Suddenly the ants jumped into close focus as if someone had pulled a zoom. They became monstrous, horrible. It happened so quickly, so nastily, that Vinny started. The jerk woke her up, instantly.

For the second time, she said, aloud, 'It was only a stupid dream.' She pushed her hair back with her fingers and thought, How quickly dreams fade! It was all so real only a moment ago: those goggle-eyed heads . . . Well, that was because I've so often looked at ants through the magnifying glass. And the Queen's commentary, that was because of TV gymnasts. And the music—

No, wait a minute! The 'music' was still going. TAP, TAP, TAP-TAP, TAP. TAP, SCRATCH, SCRAPE, TAP . . .

It came from outside. From out there. She got up, wondering why her heart was thumping, and went to the window. She turned the curved handle, swung the window wide open and craned forward to look out.

Something big, something brown or almost black,

something shining and humped and long-legged – something moved! It scuttled jerkily, glitteringly, very fast – and disappeared under the rhododendron bush.

Had she seen it? Yes. The dull-shining, spear-shaped leaves of the bush still quivered. The thing was still in there.

She ran downstairs on bare feet. The garden, the bush, she had to get out there quickly before it got away! She had to find out what it was!

At the garden door, she stopped. It was not that she was afraid. Of course not. It was just that there was coarse, sharp gravel outside and her feet were bare. You can't walk barefoot on gravel, can you?

Of course not.

Toby found an old song to do with smoke and smoking. His father had taped it from a 78.

When the last line of the song came, Toby turned up the volume . . .

Cigareets are the curse of the whole human race
A man looks a monkey with one in his face
I'm telling you, sister, I'm telling you, brother—
A FOOL AT ONE END, A FIRE AT THE
OTHER!

He was playing the song at full strength when the door of his room was flung open and Bets stormed in. 'Enough of that!' she said, pulling the plug out of the wall. The tape recorder went silent. Toby tried to look surprised and innocent. 'It's my favourite tape,' he said.

'No, it's not. It's your favourite way of getting at Aunt Craven,' Bets said.

'Honestly, Mum—'

'Never mind your honestly,' Bets said. 'Look: I'm getting sick and tired of you and Vinny ganging up on my sister, your aunt. Particularly now. She's going through a trying time.'

'Oh yes, the dying Daimler,' Toby answered, wagging his head cheekily.

Bets answered by slapping his face, hard.

Toby was amazed by this. So was his mother. The noise of the slap seemed to hover in the air while they stared at each other.

Then Bets sat down on Toby's bed and said, 'Look, she's having a bad time. Not just the Daimler, it's other things, things you wouldn't know about.'

'I thought—'

'Never mind what you thought. Think about being nice to her for a change. Both of you.'

Toby began to feel the sting of the slap. 'She's not all that easy to be nice to,' he muttered. 'Bossing everyone about.'

'She's *had* to be bossy. *Had* to be tough. You're too young—'

'Too young to understand,' Toby said, sullenly. There was a silence.

'Just be nice to her,' Bets said. 'Please.'

Toby looked at his mother's clouded face and said, 'OK, Mum. Sorry.'

She stood up, loosened her shoulders and said, smiling, 'Who's a lovely boy, then?'

'I am, Mum,' he grinned.

'You are too,' she said. They both laughed. She went downstairs, saying, 'I'll make some tea. Five minutes.'

And special herbal tea for Aunt Craven, Toby said to himself. But he added, Now, now! Be nice!

He talked to Vinny about it. She was not very interested.

'I told you so,' she said. 'It's time you laid off. Me too. Mum's right.' She was biting her lip.

Toby said, 'Aunt Craven's upset, Mum's just belted me one across the chops and now you're looking like a wet weekend. What's happening in this house?'

'Things,' Vinny said, not looking at him.

'What do you mean, things?'

'I wish I knew,' Vinny said. 'Whatever it is, it's not *in* the house, it's outside. Or in my head.'

'What are you talking about—'

'I don't know. I don't *know!*' Vinny shouted, and ran to her room, slamming the door behind her.

'Well, thank *you*,' Toby said. He put his earphones on and listened to reggae, full strength.

Chapter Six

Vinny had stopped having dreams. Now there was something worse: the Voice.

The Voice came from nowhere. It belonged to nobody. It was not male or female, high or low. And Vinny never knew when it would come.

When the Voice invaded her brain, it asked questions to which there were no answers. Such impossible questions!

'*Who is handle?*' it would demands, as she waited in the queue for school lunch.

'*When is motor-car?*' it would shout in her head in the middle of the night.

'*Why is sleeping?*'

'*Which is biggest?*'

'*What for woman man?*'

'Hearing voices – that's the first sign of madness,' Vinny said. She sat on the edge of her bed. 'No, that's wrong, talking to yourself is the first sign. That's what I am doing now. Yatter yatter yatter.' But she had to talk to herself to try and keep the Voice away.

She could feel it coming on now. Here were the sounds in her head that she always heard when the Voice was about to invade – the singing, tingling, whistling, background noises . . .

She flung herself on her bed and covered her ears with a pillow.

'*When is motor-car?*' said the Voice.

'Oh, shut up! Go away!'

'*How far the road running?*' the Voice insisted.

Vinny began crying into the pillow: weak, silly sobs. The Voice had gone on for three days and nights. She could take no more.

'*How is get out?*' said the Voice.

Vinny started screaming.

Bets was out shopping. Robbie was at work. Toby was deafening himself with reggae. Only Aunt Craven heard Vinny's screams. She ran up the stairs and into Vinny's room.

'Go away, go away, go A W A Y!' Vinny screamed at the Voice.

Aunt Craven thought, she means me. She hates me. But

she could not leave the figure in front of her, writhing on the bed, head crushed into a pillow. 'Vinny!' Aunt Craven said. 'Vinny! Look at me!'

She began stroking the back of Vinny's head. She felt awkward doing it – clumsy and empty. The children did not like her. What good could she do?

Then Vinny's arms were locked around her neck, hurting her, and Vinny's hot tears wetted her neck. 'Make them go away, please, Aunt Craven!' Vinny sobbed. 'You're strong, make them go!'

A long five minutes later, when the story of the Voices was told and Vinny's head lay quietly on her lap, Aunt Craven was glad of her strength. Strength was needed: *she* was needed.

'We'll search it out and fight it,' she told Vinny. 'We'll win, Vinny. We'll beat it, just you see!'

She saw that Vinny had fallen asleep, head on her aunt's lap, one arm round her waist. Again Aunt Craven stroked the back of Vinny's head, this time feeling neither clumsy nor empty.

'They're very big,' the Daughter Queen told the Mother Queen.

'Good. Feed them well.'

'Some are so big they cannot stand. Their legs are too thin.'

'Kill them.'

'Yes, certainly, right away. About feeding them—'

'You are to change the diet in the way I have already instructed you. To prevent weak limbs. You are to send out more hunters for more food. Animal food. Meat. There are rats and mice, rabbits, dogs and cats. Find them. Kill them.'

'Yes, Your Majesty. My hunters are already out. But the big ones are hard to kill—'

'Kill them.'

'Yes, Your Majesty. But, Your Majesty – could you tell me the best way to kill them? How do your warriors do it?'

'My warriors are small. I am small. Only you are big. I made you big.'

'Oh, Your Majesty. I see. I did not know.'

'Hunt the big animals. Kill them.'

'Yes, Your Majesty.'

The Jaguar eased to a halt nose to nose with Aunt Craven's Daimler. 'Hi!' Greg Stewkeley called to the knot of people round the old car. 'Just happened to be passing. What's the trouble?'

He had interrupted a family conference. Everyone was standing round the Daimler, wondering what to do about it.

Greg got out of his car, saw the dark oil stains in the gutter and said, 'Oh-oh! You *have* got trouble.' The bonnet was open. He looked at the engine. 'A con rod's gone through the crankcase,' he said.

'We know that,' Robbie said, coldly. 'What we don't know is what to do about it.'

'Spend a thousand smackers,' Greg said. 'A thousand *minimum*. That's supposing someone's got the parts for a heap this old.'

'A *heap*?' Aunt Craven said, staring Greg in the eye.

He wilted. 'There I go!' Greg said, forcing a big smile. 'Trust old Greg to put his foot in it! I call all cars "heaps". I call *mine* a heap, don't I Barry? This is Barry da Silva, he knows all about money.' He introduced Barry to everyone. Somehow Greg knew all the names, even Aunt Craven's. 'Whose car is it?' he asked.

'The heap,' Aunt Craven said, 'happens to belong to me.'

'Nice car,' Barry da Silva said. His eyes were taking in every detail of the old Daimler. 'The saloons, they're nothing much. But these convertibles: there's a market for the convertibles.'

'Barry knows,' Greg said, beaming.

'You want to get that Daimler working,' Barry said. 'There's a solid market.'

Robbie said, 'Tell us how.'

'Trumperley Motors. It so happens I've got a part interest. Ongoing business. There's an old boy at Trumperley's, an old-car nut, he could have the bits. He had an Alvis Silver Lady, a load of rubbish; he did it up, sold it overseas for £18,000.' He shrugged his shoulders mournfully, as if lamenting a deal that had got away from him.

'Let's get the show on the road!' Greg shouted. 'Just allow me the use of your 'phone for five minutes!'

Four minutes later, he came out of the house, rubbing his hands. 'Trumperley's will fix it!' he announced. 'Pick-up coming in the next hour! No sweat!'

'You'd better cancel it,' Aunt Craven said. 'You said a thousand pounds. I haven't got a thousand pounds for you or anyone else.'

'No, hang about, hang about!' Greg said. He and Barry held a short muttered conference. Then Greg said, 'All fixed, no sweat!'

'I doubt it,' Aunt Craven said.

'No, listen! That old boy I mentioned – the old-car nut – he's always wanted my 1951 Riley, right? My Dad's car, actually, God rest him. He'll give me £450 for the Riley, right? You give me the £450, I give the old boy the Riley, he fixes your motor for free and everyone's smiling!'

'Done!' Aunt Craven said, instantly.

Barry gave her a knowing look. 'Smart lady,' he said. 'You've got yourself a bargain. Greg's the loser.'

'Win some, lose some,' Greg said. 'Who cares!'

And that was how Greg entered the family circle and home.

His reason was soon made obvious. Beaming, he got Toby and Vinny to one side. Beaming, he asked them how they were getting on with their Mindbending. Had they made any plans? Bad. Had they talked to

79

anyone else about getting an act together? They hadn't? Good.

Vinny said, 'We've just about forgotten Mindbending. We've got other things to think of.'

'What sort of things?'

'Exams,' Toby said, gloomily.

'Ah, well, they'll soon be over,' Greg said. 'Then we can talk business, right?'

'Not me,' Vinny said.

'Why not? With talents like yours?'

Vinny looked away from Greg's smiling face. 'I've got things on my mind,' she said.

Bloggs jumped up on a little table and tried to give Vinny a friendly butt on the forehead. His head was still a mess, there were raw patches where the vet had cut away fur before stitching. Bloggs didn't seem to mind.

'What happened to the cat?' Greg said. He looked really concerned.

'That's one of the things on my mind,' Vinny replied.

'No, tell me, I want to know,' Greg said. 'How did he get those injuries?'

'We don't know. Even the vet was puzzled.'

'You know my dog, Garth, the big Alsatian? I've even been a bit worried for him! But he's a big dog, you don't take liberties with him. But your cat . . . and there're other animals. A lady down the road – her Corgi copped it. And three dead cats found so far. Bits of them, anyhow. And a little girl's rabbits.'

Vinny stared at Greg. Toby said, 'You mean, it's happening often, all over the place? But why? How?'

Then Greg said something that amazed Toby and Vinny. 'So you two don't know anything about it?' he asked, in a determined but uneasy voice.

'*Us*? Why should *we* want to hurt—' Toby began.

'The heads, the heads get left,' Greg said, speaking rapidly. 'No trace of the bodies. Just the heads left. Funny, that. And the wounds, they're not what you'd call natural.'

'But why should *we* know anything about it?' Vinny said.

'Well, I hear things. Actually, I asked around about you two. The things you can do, Mental Magic and all that. Some of your school pals said you did weird things . . . breaking glass, getting even with people. I heard something about a boy's watch.'

'But *animals!*' Vinny said, loudly. 'You can't think we'd hurt *animals!*'

'No, of course not, not unless you were sort of testing your powers, something like that. But you're not, are you?'

'Of course not!'

'You're sure?'

Vinny could have hit Greg. But then something hit her: close-up images of the ants, the formicarium; memories of the dreams, the Voice . . .

'*Oh, Your Majesty, they're so big they frighten me!*'

'You are their ruler. Rule.'

'But they're such monsters, they can't even see me. I am afraid of being trodden underfoot.'

'Instruct your guards to protect you.'

'Oh, Your Majesty, I wish I were as strong as you . . .'

The Old Queen cut off and thought, Fool! 'Not as strong as me' – how true! I am the true Queen, you are merely my messenger, my go-between. And my breeder of conquerors.

But, thought the Old Queen, weak and foolish as you are, you must not die. I cannot command my army of giants except through you. I cannot escape this prison without you. I cannot conquer but through you.

She returned to the business of making battle plans.

Chapter Seven

Suddenly, TV and newspaper people were everywhere. They were after animal stories. Toby and Vinny were stopped in the street by media people who wanted to know the way to a pub, a farm, the nearest telephone. Local people complained that they couldn't get a drink in the pubs – the media people crowded the bars.

Greg Stewkeley did not complain. He knew the district, he knew the locals – and he talked freely and fast. The media people pounced on him and bought him drinks. They were doing it now, at The Rifleman . . .

'Sheep?' Greg said. 'Oh, yes. Ned Cutler – the farmer over there, I'll introduce you later – he's lost five sheep and one more last night makes six. (Oh, ta muchly, here's mud in your eye.)

'Bad boys? Yobbos? No, they're not responsible for the killings. Ask *her*, Mrs Randall. Yes, that lady in the corner. No wonder she looks miserable, they got her Corgi. Yes, the same kind of injuries, nothing an animal or human would go in for. (Well, just a small one, then, with plain water.)

'You want my opinion, do you? I'm in the scientific line, right? I don't go in for opinions, I go in for *facts*. Facts and fact-finding. And I've got the equipment to do it: electronic equipment, gear that measures and records. Scientifically. Could be useful, don't you think? Well, yes, we could fix up a chat, I suppose. Here's my card. Call in any time at my office.'

Vinny said, 'I don't like Bloggs going out even in the daytime, not after all the things that have been happening. The poor animals . . .'

Aunt Craven said, 'I'll go with him in the garden. Keep an eye on him while he does his duty. He'll be all right. And anyway, the attacks don't seem to happen in the daytime. Always at night.' She stroked Bloggs. He liked the way she stroked – very decisively and vigorously. His bandages were all gone now and his shaven patches showed new fur.

'If only we knew,' Aunt Craven said, 'what or who *does* these things! I'd give them something to think about!'

Vinny looked away.

'And why,' Aunt Craven continued, 'it's only *here*,

nowhere else in the country. It's as if a crowd of maniacs had got loose.'

Vinny said nothing.

Vinny went to the formicarium. She leaned over it, chin in hands, and said, 'Talk to me.'

The ants in the formicarium scurried about their mysterious business, moving no faster and no slower than usual.

'I want the Queen,' Vinny said – using her voice softly and her mind loudly. 'Speak to me! Go on, speak to me!'

No answer came from the ants. The Queen could not be seen.

You're always talking to *me*, you know you are! Vinny's mind shouted. Asking stupid questions! Never leaving me alone! Why won't you speak to me now?

The ants went on being busy at their own pace.

It *is* you, isn't it? her mind demanded. It's got to be you, it can't be anyone else! And you're killing the animals, aren't you? I don't know how or why you do it, but you *do* do it, I know you do! So talk to me! Explain!

The ants went about their ceaseless business, ignoring her.

Yet, half an hour later, the Voice bored into her mind again, asking yet another question. '*Glass is strong, glass strong?*' it wanted to know.

The question sounded almost sensible. Vinny refused to answer it. Go away, go away! her mind shrieked.

Toby saw her shadowed face. He said, 'I wish you'd tell me what's on your mind.' He was half angry, half worried.

Vinny said, 'I'm just worried, that's all. I'm allowed to be worried sometimes, aren't I?'

'Worried about what? It's something to do with crazy Aunt Craven, isn't it?'

'Aunt Craven is not crazy. Aunt Craven's *all right*. She's not the same inside as she is outside. We're friends.'

Toby raised one eyebrow in his Man of the World expression but Vinny was not looking at him. 'Friends, eh?' he said. 'That's something new. Well, if it's not Aunt Craven, what is it? Something to do with Mindbending?'

'We haven't done any Mindbending for days,' Vinny said.

'Weeks, more like,' Toby said. 'We ought to start again, Vinny; we were getting it going really well.'

'No!' Vinny said, sharply.

'Seriously, I've been thinking about it a lot. I've got an idea for an *act*. Something that would knock them dead!'

'*No!*' Vinny almost shouted.

Toby ignored her. 'Listen,' he said. 'Remember the Mystical Mouse we made for Bloggs? Well, suppose we got together an act concentrated on animals. Nothing but animals. Just imagine it! There we are in front of the TV cameras, and there's lots of coloured drums and boxes, like elephants have at circuses, but smaller. And there's soft, mysterious music in the background.'

'I don't want to hear it,' Vinny said.

'No, *listen*. Then *I* say, "What sort of animal would you like over there, Vinny?" And *you* say – you're dressed in a leotard thing with lots of spangles – *you* say, "I'd like to see a dear little mouse! No, a whole family of mice!" Then we Mindbend like mad, and there they are, the mice, all spotlit! Big sensation! Then we go on to bigger animals.'

'No!' Vinny shouted. She came at Toby, hitting out at him with useless fists. 'Stop it!' she shouted.

She gave up the attack and started crying. They were in her bedroom. Toby led her to the bed and sat beside her with an arm round her. 'What's up, Vinny?' he said, quietly.

'We've done something dreadful!' she choked.

'Go on, sis. Something dreadful?'

'It's all my fault,' she sobbed. 'I was always better at it than you . . . Mindbending, I mean.'

'Yes, that's true. What's so dreadful about that?'

'I spent hours at it,' she said. 'Hours and hours, staring at the ants in the formicarium, until my brain was full of them. And they seemed to get bigger and bigger, because I was so close to them, I suppose.'

'No need to cry,' he said.

'And then I had an accident with them, I never told you. I dropped the formicarium, some ants got out. And I mended it, but some ants got away.'

'They're only ants,' Toby said. 'Just a few little ants.'

'But don't you see! I was seeing them *big*. I was *thinking* them big!'

'So what? The ants haven't changed, they're still as tiny as ever. Come over here. Look at them! Look at the formicarium!'

'I don't want to look. I won't look.'

'Well, all right, don't look. Just take my word for it, they're tiny.'

'But they,' Vinny said, 'aren't *the ants that escaped!*'

She had lifted her face to stare at him with wet, guilty eyes. 'The animals,' she said. 'All the animals that have been attacked. Some of them killed. Don't you see? It's the ants! The giant ants I made! It must be them doing it!'

Toby forced a laugh. 'Is that what you've been worrying about all this time!' he said. 'Listen! There're no such things as giant ants. And even if there were, you couldn't have done it! I mean, we can make a Mystical Mouse, a sort of ghost; but we can't make anything *real*. Honestly, Vin! You couldn't make a giant ant if you tried!'

She would not listen. 'I've done something dreadful, I know it!' she said.

'All right, then,' Toby said. 'You've created Giant Killer Ants. Fine. Let's see you do it again!'

She shook her head so violently that her hair flew.

'No, come on, Vinny, come on! Both of us together!' He had to pull and drag her to the formicarium. At first, she struggled and cried. Minutes later, however, she was absorbed in Mindbending. 'Come on!' she muttered. 'Grow . . . !'

The Mother Queen saw the white blobs looming above her. She felt their mind waves surging into her brain. The waves excited and annoyed her.

'I am busy,' she told the waves. 'Go away.' But the waves strengthened until they became a vibrating hum that shook her armoured head. She got rid of them by off-loading them throughout her colony. Ants scrabbled and tumbled as the waves hit them. The Mother Queen was left in peace until she received a call from the Daughter Queen.

'Yes?' said the Mother Queen.

'Everything is in order, Your Majesty. Just as you commanded. So I thought I ought to ask you *when.*'

'When I tell you. Not before. But very soon. You say everything is prepared? The scouts have fully explored the territory? The warriors are fighting fit?'

'Oh yes, Your Majesty! And very anxious to get started. It is quite hard to hold them back, they even attack each other sometimes. That is why I asked *when.*'

'Soon. Send out still more warrior parties to kill animals: the warriors must smell blood and flesh. Ensure that your workers give the warriors the best of the food. But don't *overfeed* the warriors. They must be hungry, angry, fierce.'

'Certainly, Your Majesty.'

'Very well, then.'

The Mother Queen cut off. Above her, the white blobs – she had almost forgotten their presence – suddenly lifted away and dwindled. Then a smothering blackness descended.

The Mother Queen went on with her battle plans.

Toby smoothed the black cover over the formicarium and said, 'There you are, Vin. We both tried like mad, and nothing happened. No giant ants.'

'Perhaps I wasn't concentrating properly, I was upset.'

'You were Mindbending like mad, don't deny it. So was I. I wish you wouldn't nibble your lower lip like that, it makes you look like a rabbit.'

'I don't know, I just don't know,' she said. She stopped nibbling and thought. What *had* she seen that day? What was the thing that scuttled into the rhododendron bush, hiding itself, making the leaves quiver? Did it *have* to be a giant ant? Why couldn't it have been a left-over picture from her own mind, or a puff of wind, or a cat?

'Come on, Vinny!' Toby said. He was standing over her, with his hands on his hips. 'Tell me all the fuss is over. Say it!'

'All over?' she said, uncertainly.

'Yes. Say it! Say "All over!"'

'All over!' she said at last. And for the first time in days, smiled and laughed.

*   *   *

At that moment, Greg Stewkeley was pushing his way through a knot of people standing round something on the ground in the car park. 'All right!' Greg said. 'Make way, let's have a look at him.'

'I found him hidden between two cars, Mr Stewkeley,' a man said. 'I heard this noise and there he was, poor old fellow.'

Greg bent down and said, 'Garth! Garth! Come on, old boy, you're all right. Open your eyes, look at me!' The big dog flapped its tail and opened one eye.

Without another word, Greg carried the Alsatian to the Jaguar and drove to the vet's. The vet said, 'He'll be all right, he's big and strong. But all these lacerations, I just don't understand it. Something's been tearing at him. Sheep, cats, and now your dog.'

Greg said, 'Garth! You're all right, aren't you? 'Course you are. I'll find them, boy, never you fear. I'll find them and get them.'

He left the vet, drove back to his office and called in his secretary. Together they went through a heap of leaflets and specification sheets. 'Put this one in my briefcase,' he said, grimly. 'Make a note for the files that I've taken it. And this one, the ultra-violet tracer. Now, who do we know who deals in electric fencing? Get them on the blower. No, get me Vince first.'

Silently, she dialled an internal number.

'Vince?' Greg said. 'Greg here. You know the Mark 2

91

cattle probe? Yeah. Well, what would happen if we ran it at mains voltage, instead of the powerpack? Blow your ears off, would it? Right. Would it *take* mains voltage? How many have we got? Only a dozen? Well, put them in the boot of my car. Get someone to adapt them for mains voltage first. Yes, I know about the law. You know what you can do with the law.'

'The electric-fencing people,' his secretary said. She handed him a telephone.

Later, he made a general call through the P A system. In every department, they heard his voice. 'Greg Stewkeley speaking,' the voice boomed. 'Anyone wants overtime for a couple of evenings and nights, report by 'phone to my secretary. Normal rates times two and a half. Outdoor clothing and gumboots. Meet in the car park 8.30. You'll have an interesting night, I promise you. *And* normal rates times two and a half.'

The Mother Queen called the Daughter Queen. 'Is everything ready?'

'Yes, Your Majesty. I think so. The warriors are very restless and vicious. Some workers have been attacked and eaten.'

'Good. All the better for the success of the operation.'

'The operation, Your Majesty?'

'Try not to be stupid. The attack, tonight. Tonight's

attack. The warriors will destroy everything that lies between them and their objective.'

'Their objective, Your Majesty?'

'Myself. The objective is my liberation. When I am freed from my prison, new queens will be bred. The new queens will extend my empire by a series of colonies extending limitlessly.'

'Yes, Your Majesty. It will be glorious.'

'It will indeed. Our race will reign supreme. No other species will be permitted to survive except as providers of food for ourselves. And I myself—'

'You will reign over us, Your Majesty. In glory.'

The Mother Queen cut off. She felt a consuming and enormous excitement. She vibrated with it. Her servant ants caught waves of her passion and tumbled, scuttered, gyrated, scrambled or just ran, blindly, touching heads, passing on the great news.

It was simply a coincidence that Greg Stewkeley had decided that, on this night, he would mount some sort of offensive against whatever creatures had attacked Garth and the other animals.

Had the Mother Queen known of his plans, she would have ignored them. She was the Queen. She would conquer ferociously; be raised in glory to her new throne; rule for ever through an endless succession of new queens, each inspired by her vision and wisdom.

The world was hers. Or soon would be.

Chapter Eight

That night, there were two sorts of storm: one outside, and one in Vinny's head.

Outside, the wind gusted – howled – blasted. Inside in her bed, Vinny's mind was stormed by the Voice. *Why is?* it asked, again and again.

Vinny pulled her pillow over her head and begged for quiet.

But the Voice was right inside her, there was no defence against it.

'*Danger is?*' it demanded.

'Go away, leave me alone! What do you mean, "Danger is?"'

'*Tree divide danger is?*' said the Voice.

It asked the question so many times that Vinny at last

understood what it could mean. 'The tree is old,' she said. 'Half dead. That's why it's divided: falling in half: *split*. Now will you be quiet?'

'*Danger when?*' said the Voice.

'Oh, leave my mind alone! You're the formicarium, aren't you? Yes, you are! You're the Queen! Admit it!'

'*Tree split danger when?*' said the Voice.

'You're the Queen!' Vinny accused. 'It's got to be you! And if it *is* you, what do you care about the tree? You're *indoors*, in the formicarium! It's *out there*, in the garden! You keep saying "Danger", there's no danger to you even if it breaks and falls!'

'*Breaking falling?*' the Voice demanded.

'Yes! Yes! On your head, I hope!'

'*Danger when?*' the Voice said.

Vinny could stand no more. She leapt from her bed and ran to Toby's room. The howling wind must have troubled his sleep, for he woke instantly and completely. Vinny flung herself on his bed and cried, 'Help me, Toby! The Voice! The Queen won't leave me alone!'

Later, when she was quiet, he said, 'All right, now? Not hearing voices any more?'

'I'm all right when I'm with you.'

''Course you are. Big Brother Bashes Baddies, OK?'

'OK. Well, half OK. The wind, listen to the wind! I hate it! Especially when the tree creaks like that.'

Toby was silent for some time; then he said, 'Why should the Queen worry about the tree? I mean, she's here, the tree's out there.'

'You'll only laugh at me,' Vinny said. 'But I'll tell you what I think. The escaped ants are somewhere very near that tree and the Queen's worried about what will happen if the tree falls and kills the ants.'

'The *giant* ants,' Toby said, mockingly. 'Don't forget they're king-sized. According to you.'

'Giant or not, I think she's worried about them. She's in touch with them somehow. Well, why not? She's certainly in touch with me!'

Toby changed the subject. 'The Queen – if it *was* the Queen, which I *don't* admit – she started by saying, "Divide", didn't she? When she meant "split"?'

'Yes. Until I corrected her.'

Toby said, 'It's a chestnut tree, a conker tree. You could make a joke out of it.'

'You could, I couldn't,' Vinny said.

'Divide and conker!' Toby said. 'Get it?' He shook her shoulder. 'Go on,' he said. 'Laugh!'

Dutifully, she said, 'Ha, ha.'

The Daughter Queen communicated with the Mother Queen. 'Oh, please, Your Majesty!' she said. 'I am so frightened! The tree above us, it is swaying and making dreadful noises!'

'Are your warriors assembled?' the Mother Queen said.

'Yes, Your Majesty. But the ground is shaking, earth is falling, tunnels are collapsing!'

'Have your workers cleared the tunnels? Kill all useless males and use their bodies to shore up weakened tunnels.'

'I have already done so, Your Majesty. But if the roots move any more and the earth crumbles – if the tree falls – if everything collapses—'

'I understand. Very well,' said the Mother Queen. 'Give the command.'

'Which command, Your Majesty?'

'Fool! The command to attack! To conquer!'

'Yes, Your Majesty. But don't you think—'

'Be silent. I will give the order myself!'

And from the mind of the Mother Queen, the great command went forth. It thrilled and stung, pierced and electrified. Workers became frantic. Warriors reared, grated their jaws, tested the surge of their chemical poisons.

Then they swung their lowered heads towards the Mother Queen's signal, and thrust their way upwards and outwards into the great windy darkness of Out There, where their target loomed: the big box standing dark against the turbulent sky, the house of the enemy.

The house stood black and enormous. The warriors did not care. They were hungry and the box held food. They were fearless – there was no word in their language for

97

fear. They were invincible – the Voice of the Mother Queen told them so.

And they were powerful. Each warrior ant was bigger than a cat – but much better armed and armoured.

The great army ran towards the house and the living food it contained.

Aunt Craven woke several times during the night. It was the wind. Branches of a shrub rattled and tapped beneath her bedroom window. The old chestnut in the garden creaked loudly enough to be heard above the buffetings and surgings of the gale. The house itself made small, uneasy noises. So she woke; but she sternly told herself to go back to sleep – and tried to obey.

This time, however, sleep would not stay. 'Blast!' she said. She switched on her bedside light, muttering, 'Stupid, fiddly switch.' She sat up and reached for one of her Daughters of the Tabernacle journals. But the printed words blurred as she read them. The wind seemed to tumble her thoughts in a mental mixer. She felt isolated, disturbed, fixed in time.

'Cats get the wind up their tails,' she said aloud. It was quite true. Even respectable Bloggs had behaved strangely during the evening – she had seen him in the garden, suddenly running furiously with his tail up, then standing still and twitching.

She threw the magazine aside and reached for the *Financial Times.* She could not read this either. There was a car advertisement and immediately her mind flicked to thoughts of her car. The Daimler would be ready in less than a week. Meanwhile, she had the Renault 5 Greg Stewkeley had lent to her, charging almost nothing. Strange man, she thought: just *what* was he after? Popularity? Having his finger in every pie? Or was it something to do with Toby and Vinny?

Toby and Vinny. Vinny and the ants . . . That was strange too. *Most* strange.

She turned off the light, closed her eyes, lay straight and concentrated on Relaxing. The Wave of Relaxation. You had to spread it upwards, inch by inch, starting with your toes. Slowly, the Wave spread up to her rib cage . . .

But the wind howled, the tappings and scrapings became louder, the Wave was not working.

Tap, scrape, tap tap tap . . . and voices, surely?

'Blast!' she said. She got out of bed, put on her dressing-gown and prepared to go downstairs. A cup of tea, that was the answer.

She walked softly along the landing. Her hand torch showed the way. She saw a line of light under Toby's bedroom and – yes – she *had* heard voices: Toby and Vinny were talking. She knocked and went in.

'Couldn't sleep!' she announced. 'I'm going to make tea. Would you two like some?'

Then she saw Vinny's disturbed face, and Toby's expression, guarded and anxious. 'Something up?' Aunt Craven asked. 'If it's private, I'll be on my way.'

'The Voice,' Vinny said. 'It's been talking at me again.' Toby made a small, surprised noise. Vinny said to him, 'It's all right, Aunt Craven knows all about it.'

Aunt Craven stood awkwardly, waiting for Vinny to say more. Vinny stayed silent. Aunt Craven said, 'Tea, then. I'll go downstairs.'

As she spoke, another sound came: a loud sound – no, two sounds! First a long-drawn-out scraping, then a sort of whirring chirrup.

'That's not the wind!' Toby said. He stood up.

'Bloggs?' Vinny said. 'No, it can't be. He's in the kitchen, in his box.'

Glass broke: a feeble tinkle but very close.

Toby ran to the window, thrust aside the curtains and looked out. 'Nothing outside,' he said. 'Hang on, I'll take a proper look.'

He opened the window. The force of the wind almost tore the handle from his grasp. The curtains streamed out, flapping. 'Nothing!' he said. 'No, wait . . .'

He gasped and drew back from the window. 'Give me your torch, Aunt Craven,' he said, shakily. He shone the torch downwards.

'Wake Dad and Mum,' he said. 'Quickly!' He threw the torch to Aunt Craven and went rushing down the stairs.

He had no trouble finding the source of the tinkling sound: a broken window pane in the kitchen door. It was a small, corner pane. He bent to examine the jagged hole, but drew back: he glimpsed something that moved, something shiny, browny-black – something that shouldn't have been there. Something bad. He did not want to see it properly.

'Other door,' he muttered. He backed away from the glass-paned door and through the proper, wooden kitchen door. Between the two doors there was a very small porch, cluttered with gumboots and garden things. He thought, It doesn't matter if they break the glass-paned door to pieces; it's the strong wooden door that matters. He threw the garden tools into the kitchen, and locked and bolted the door.

His father had the big torch and was shining it into the garden. Lights were on all over the house and it was easy to see outside.

There were twenty or thirty of them, in the garden. Maybe more.

The Mother Queen said, 'Pull yourself together. Tell me what you are doing. Or failing to do.'

'Oh, please, Your Majesty, it is terrible! The tree is going to fall! I will be killed!'

'Fool!' said the Mother Queen. 'Who cares if you live or die?'

'Oh! There it goes again! That awful groaning tearing noise!'

'The *warriors!*' said the Mother Queen. 'Why are they not moving forward? Why aren't they in action?'

'Oh ... the warriors ... The scouts have already gone

forward, Your Majesty. They are in the target area. They tested the defences, they broke something and they say they can get inside. The whole army could find a way in, they say.'

'Then why isn't the whole army advancing?'

'It's so terrible here, Your Majesty! So difficult! Some of the warriors can't get out, the earth moves when the tree moves, tunnels are falling in all the time, many warriors are trapped. They are digging their way out with the help of the workers but – Oh! Bits of the tree are falling down!'

'Incompetent weakling!' said the Mother Queen.

Aunt Craven said, 'Why do they just *stand* there, moving their horrible legs and waving their horrible heads? What are they *waiting* for?'

Bets said, 'How many have you counted, Toby?'

'About forty, I think. But I suppose there could be hundreds more. We can't really see.' His voice was high and unsteady.

Bets said, 'There must be something we can do! Weapons we could use . . . We've got to keep them *out*! If they ever get in, we're done for. The size of them!'

Their torches lit the giant ants, spotlighting lowered, wagging heads with vibrating antennae; glinting limbs that moved incessantly but not yet with a set purpose; humped, armoured bodies that seemed to be pumping something inside them – supplies of poison? Formic acid?

Occasionally the lens of an eye caught the light and threw it back as a meaningless, uncaring disc of light.

Ants and humans waited, none of them knowing for what. The wind howled, the tree groaned, the minutes dragged.

Then came a vast, rending squawk and a long, drawnout crash that shook the house.

'The chestnut tree!' Toby said. 'It's come down!'

The crash of the falling tree was followed by a smash of breaking glass. 'That's *them*,' Robbie muttered. 'The ants. They're attacking. Through a window. Sounded like the french window. Come on, Toby!'

They ran to the french window that led from the dining room into the garden. They found only one expanse of glass broken. A branch of the chestnut tree had been caught by the wind and hurled through the glass. 'No ants, Dad,' Toby said. He had expected to see waving legs and thrusting heads, not this wet, tired-looking branch, looking as untidily familiar as the room itself.

'I'll switch the lights on,' Robbie said. 'See what's been damaged.'

Vinny appeared at the door of the room, like a ghost. 'Don't,' she said. Her eyes were wide. Her arms hung limply at her side. 'No lights,' she said.

Toby ran to her and seized her hand. It was cold. 'Vinny?' he said, as if trying to wake a sleepwalker.

'No lights. Lights guide them.' Her expression was as

frozen as her hand. She tossed her head fretfully and shouted, 'I don't want to hear! *Just go away!*'

Toby gently pulled at her hand and said, 'Vinny! Talk to me!'

She half heard him and said, 'She keeps going on at me, talking and talking. The Queen . . .'

'What is she telling you?'

'She says, "Warriors, attack!" She won't stop saying it, my head's full of her! Stupid old cow!' She had become for the moment a peevish little girl.

Aunt Craven ran into the room. 'We've got to get organized!' she shouted. Then she saw Vinny's face, and, as Toby had done, became quiet. 'Vinny? Vinny?' she said, and took the girl's free hand. 'Is it the Queen, Vinny?'

'She's always nagging away at me,' Vinny whined. 'She thinks she owns me.'

'You're sure it's the Queen, Vinny? It's important to be sure.'

'Oh, it's her all right!' Vinny said. 'She keeps saying "Attack!"' She shook her head uncertainly, as if shaking off her little-girl state. 'I'm sure it's her,' she said in her normal voice.

Bets was at the door. 'They're beginning to move!' she said. 'More and more of them!'

Robbie swore. 'Weapons,' he grunted. Toby said, 'Garden tools, Dad. In the kitchen. I'll come with you.'

They collected the tools and handed them out. Hoes, an axe, a rake, a chopper, a scythe.

They went to the windows. In the light of their torches, they saw giant ants everywhere: hundreds of them, all moving fast, all advancing on the house.

'No lights, no torches!' Vinny said.

In the darkness, they readied themselves for the attack.

Chapter Nine

Half a mile away on the trading estate, Greg Stewkeley said to Barry da Silva, 'Don't wave it about like that, hold it steady while I hammer it in.' The hammer came down; Barry, holding the stake, winced.

Around them, lanterns showed a dozen human figures. They made strange shapes in the shifting light. More than half Greg's workforce had turned out to earn big overtime and enjoy an adventure in the night: a campaign against whatever it was that attacked animals. Stakes were driven in, lengths of cable uncoiled, generators started, cattle probes – and some cleverer devices – tested. It would have been good fun but for the gale. But even that was exciting.

Barry said, 'Watch out for my hands! I'm not cut out

for this sort of thing.' The hammer came down: he winced. 'And anyhow,' he said, 'you're probably wasting time.'

Greg said, 'We'll have a whole ring of stakes like this, right? Then we staple the live wire across. Anything that runs into it – PFFZZ! Look out!'

Barry said, 'That's what I mean. Waste of time. Why should the whatever-it-is want to come *here* to be electrocuted? Why not a dozen other places?'

'They got Garth here,' Greg said, grimly. 'And this is my place.'

'But what about all the other places? For instance, what about the house where those kids live – the Mental Magic kids? They're the only ones who've been doing mysterious things. Things to do with insects and animals.'

Greg rested his hammer, stared at Barry and said, 'Say that again, slowly. No, don't! Let me think!'

He thought; then threw his hammer down and began running towards his car, shouting orders over his shoulder as he went.

'The kids! Of course!' he said, as he shut the door of the Jaguar.

The french window had to be sealed off somehow. One big pane of glass was already gone, and the others could easily be broken by the ants. 'The grille, the anti-burglar thing,' Robbie said.

Toby knew what he meant straight away. Years ago, Robbie had bought a big anti-burglary grille that covered the whole window area. It locked in place from the inside. 'I'll get it,' Toby said.

'You can't,' said his father. 'It's propped against the toolshed. You're not going out there.'

'I'll be all right,' Toby said. His father turned away to shift a chair that might help block the broken window. When he turned back, Toby was gone, running down the path.

'Come back, don't be a fool!' Robbie shouted. Toby heard but ran on.

Toby could barely see. The storm clouds rushed across the moon, moonlight came and went. He peered into the bluish darkness, looking for humped, shining shapes. 'I can't see any of them,' he muttered. But he could see the shed, quite clearly and very close.

There it was! The grille! His hands recognized the wide square mesh. He pulled at it. It stuck. Why? Brambles, bricks? He pulled, it flexed and moved. One corner was free, pull harder—

Something moved, very fast, close. A live thing that glinted. An awful coldness seized Toby inside. He gave a kind of sob and pulled and tugged frantically at the grille. But the moving thing was closer.

It seemed to leave the ground and *fly* at him. It was bouncing at him—

The grille came free. Toby fell backwards. The grille fell over him. The thing's jaws squeaked as they bit the steel mesh.

His father was suddenly there, shouting, flailing with the scythe, hitting out savagely.

And then it was all over, they were back in the house – Toby never remembered running there – and his father's eyes were frightened and staring, his mouth was moving.

When Robbie could speak, he said, 'You shouldn't – have done – that.' Toby started laughing and could not stop, even while he helped his father clamp the grille.

When it was in place, Robbie said, 'Well . . . this is now just about the safest place in the house. They can't get through *that!*' He gave the grille a backhanded slap. It rattled and something caught in the square of mesh shook free and fell on the carpet.

It was the severed foreleg of a huge ant.

Toby stopped laughing to be sick.

'I think I'm going to be sick,' Bets told Aunt Craven when the big window in the kitchen was smashed in and the shiny, clawed legs waved and poked at them.

Aunt Craven said, 'Sick my eye,' and slashed at the legs and head with the big carving knife. 'Like cutting corn,' she bellowed. The hole in the window was crowded with heads and limbs, legs and antennae. She hit out almost blindly at them, not wanting to see what each knife stroke produced: limbs that still flexed, severed antennae that still twitched.

'Help me!' she shouted to Bets. 'There're too many

of them! If the rest of the window caves in, we've had it!'

Bets, bent double with nausea, jabbed at the ants with a garden rake. 'Watch what you're doing!' shouted Aunt Craven. 'Don't smash any more of the window!' But Bets hardly heard. She was almost in shock. She prodded the invading ants feebly.

'For heaven's sake,' Aunt Craven shouted at her, 'don't just tickle them! Smash them! And mind the glass!'

Vinny stumbled in, carrying a folding card-table. 'Out of my way!' she muttered. With Aunt Craven's help, she covered the window with the table. 'It's not big enough, there's still a gap, they'll get in!' Vinny shouted.

'Never mind that, it's better than before,' Aunt Craven replied. 'How do we hold it in place? We can't stand here holding it up forever.'

Vinny said, 'Clothes-line.' There were curtain-rail brackets above the window and radiators below. Somehow they lashed the table in place. 'It won't hold,' Vinny said.

'It will give me a rest,' Aunt Craven said, stabbing at the little space not covered by the table.

Toby was upstairs, securing windows and making sure that no ants had climbed up the walls.

A single ant suddenly made faces at him from the other side of the window. It must have jumped from a nearby lilac tree. Toby shouted with fright. The ant scrambled furiously to find a grip, its great head rocking; then it fell backwards into darkness.

Toby took a stupid chance; he opened the window and looked out. Beneath him there was a ring of glinting bodies, all furiously active. They made a moving skirt round the walls of the house. The bodies moved with hysterical speed, getting in each other's way, climbing over each other, even falling on their backs and waving their legs. Some ants were attacking a bush, tearing at its branches, snapping at the harmless leaves. 'Hysterical,' Toby muttered. 'Fighting mad.'

In the distance, he could just make out columns of support: lines of ants, all advancing. As the lines neared the house, they divided into narrow strings.

'Divide and conquer!' Toby said, the words jumping into his mind. 'Of course!'

He ran downstairs to get to Vinny, the formicarium – and the Queen.

Greg brought the Jaguar to a sliding halt, flung open the door, left it open, and started running to the house.

The house was dark but the concrete path leading to the front door gleamed brightly. He ran up it – tripped over something that appeared from nowhere, something that could have been a football – and fell so hard that he saw stars. The concrete had scraped the skin of the palm of his left hand. He sat up and stared at the hand, trying to pull himself together.

His hand hurt. No, wait – the real pain came, not from his hand, but from the calf of his leg. A sharp, biting pain – but the thing that tripped him had not been sharp.

And then the pain came again but much worse this time. A bite – a stab – he was being attacked! He got up and stood, swaying. He felt a wetness on the back of one hand, and then on his thigh, soaking through his trousers. And then, for the third time, an agonizing pain in his leg.

He tottered, spun round, swore and began kicking out wildly, dazed by pain, the furious wind and a lancing fear. The fear became panic when he saw them: the great ants all around him, running towards him, jaws working, legs like jointed machines. He waved his arms like a scarecrow, kicked out in a frenzy and lurched down the path to the place of safety: the Jaguar, the welcoming car with its calm little lights on the dashboard, its soft leather seats.

He more or less fell into the driver's seat. He must have left something on the seat; he felt it crush under his weight . . . Never mind, slam the door, get the engine started, get out.

But the thing he had sat on heaved and stirred beneath him. And another thing was in the back of the car: it was rearing up, it was going to attack!

He screamed, flung himself from the car and ran to the house. He would hammer on the door, someone would let him in, he'd be safe. But the ants were everywhere!

They ringed the house, he would never reach the door! They were waiting to spring on him – to tear him with their sharp jaws, to squirt poison into him, to pull him down and smother him!

Once again he ran. Now he was sobbing and sightless. He staggered on until, with a rib-cracking impact, he ran into a car. The Renault. The car he had lent the Craven woman. It stood on the gravel patch, away from the house.

He wrenched at the door handle. 'For God's sake, don't be locked!' The door swung open. He was inside, he was safe, the car was his fortress. He leaned his head on the steering wheel and sobbed.

Outside, *they* scraped and tapped and rustled, trying to get in. 'Fooled you!' Greg shouted, laughing drunkenly. 'Can't get in, see?'

And I can't get out, he thought. I can't get away. Unless she's left the key in the ignition . . .

He looked and groped. No key. In the glove locker, then? The key was there.

The engine started first time. He blessed it. An ant jumped on to the bonnet and waved its antennae at him through the windscreen. He cursed it. He switched on the headlamps. There were ants everywhere, the sight of them sickened and terrified him; the lights seemed to attract them, their heads swung towards him.

He sat back and said, 'Calm. Calm right down, right? Everything nice and easy.'

The sound of his own words and the car's engine cheered him. He became more than calm: now he was savagely determined. Deliberately, he took in the lie of the land. The lawn was level with the paths. He could drive round half the house if he wanted to.

'Right,' he said. 'Your old pal Greg's on his way.'

He engaged first gear.

Chapter Ten

Toby found Vinny in the kitchen. She was methodically striking a hoe into the heads and limbs of ants trying to squeeze past the card-table. The effect of her blows was so disgusting that Toby felt squeamish. Vinny simply looked tired. 'You take over,' she said. 'I've had enough.'

'Vinny, listen! I've had a Divide-and-Conquer idea! We've got to use the formicarium – get to the Queen—'

'There's no time for messing about Mindbending,' she replied. 'We've got to defend the house.'

'But, Vinny, listen! Let's create Mental Magic animals! Lots of them! The ants will go for them instead of us! Divide and Conquer!'

To his surprise, she said, 'All right. But we've got to do it here. Get the formicarium.'

He put it on a table behind them, well away from the window. '*Mindbenders!*' he hissed. 'Come on, Vinny! Hard as you can go!'

'What sort of animals?' she said, tiredly.

'Rabbits! Lots of them. In the garden. Here, I'll take the hoe, you concentrate on concentrating.'

She seemed too tired to argue. She bent over the formicarium, head in hands. Toby had to force himself. Her eyes were already closed and her lips moved.

He could not know that she was already in contact with the Mother Queen.

It was a new sort of contact: now the Voice was garbled, it came and went. For Vinny, it was like talking through a crossed wire . . .

'*Attack, attack!*' shouted the Mother Queen.

RABBITS, said Vinny's mind. Lots of rabbits. Not tame ones, wild ones. All over the garden.

'*What?*' said the Mother Queen. '*Where are the rest of the warriors? Has the first wave broken through the defences? Answer me!*'

RABBITS, thought Vinny.

'Oh, Your Majesty, it's very difficult. Many warriors are still trapped. Some are still freeing themselves,' said the Daughter Queen.

RABBITS all over the garden, Vinny thought.

'*Don't talk to me of rabbits!*' said the Mother Queen. '*Talk to me of slaughter, glory, victory!*'

'But Your Majesty—'

RABBITS.
'*What? What? What?*'

Toby cleared a space with the hoe and had time to look out of the window. 'It's worked!' he told Vinny. 'They're everywhere!'

Most of the rabbits seemed stunned. Many sat on their hind legs, front paws dangling, looking about them with puzzled, bulging eyes.

Hundreds of ants saw them, forgot their true target and swarmed to attack this easy prey. Antennae waved, eyes glistened, jaws opened wide.

Yet when the merciless mouths snapped shut they closed on – nothing! Or on something that was for an instant fur and warm flesh, yet the next instant a memory.

Then the ants milled around the fading fantasy, climbed over each other to get to the zero in their midst, even snapped at each other in fury.

'*Attack! The warriors must not weaken!*'
'But Your Majesty—'
RABBITS.

Greg let in the clutch and the little Renault's tyres spun. Then they gripped and the car lurched and bumped over gravel and grass, faster and faster.

The headlights made everything easy. They picked out grave, disciplined strings of ants advancing on the house:

Greg drove through them. They showed tumbling clusters of ants, attacking something invisible: Greg charged the clusters and crushed bodies went flying.

'This one's for you, Garth!' Greg muttered as the Renault's front wing ploughed through masses of jostling ants fringing the walls of the house. 'Nice one,' Greg said. 'Right: first gear . . . hard down on your right, aim over there . . . plenty of revs . . . second . . . whoomph! Did you hear that, Garth? Did you feel it? *They* felt it all right!'

When the ground was littered with crushed and smashed bodies, he stopped the car to rest and think. He'd killed thousands of ants: good. But there seemed always to be thousands more. Look over there, by the fallen tree! They were still coming out of the ground, still forming running lines. How many of them *were* there?

And the ants he had missed – they didn't seem bothered by anything. That lot over there, they're climbing over each other to reach the window, doing everything in such an organized way.

He lit a small cigar, engaged first and headed the Renault for the pyramid forming at the window.

Crunch.

Aunt Craven ran into the kitchen and said, 'You two all right? Great. We're holding on. I've checked upstairs, the ants can't seem to climb the walls. Otherwise we'd be in real trouble.'

Toby said, 'I keep hearing a car engine.'

'That's your pal Greg Stewkeley, he's going great guns. Running the Renault up and down the garden, *steamrolling* the blighters. Hope he doesn't run out of petrol. I put three gallons in yesterday.'

She turned to Vinny, saw her face and paused. 'Vinny!' she said. 'Something up?'

'She's been making magical rabbits,' Toby said, coolly. Mindbending had left him tired and cross. 'Me too. Quite a strain, you'd be surprised.' He poked the hoe into the latest crush of ants thrusting through the card-table gap. He hated doing it.

'You've been doing *what*?'

'Making rabbits. Mindbending them. That's why things have quietened down. But you don't believe in Mental Magic and stuff like that, do you, Aunt?'

Aunt Craven's lower lip stuck out angrily. 'Are you trying to be cheeky?' she said.

'Well, you must have seen them when you were looking out upstairs. Didn't you see the ants behaving strangely? Attacking things for no reason?'

'Yes,' said Aunt Craven, looking stunned. 'But that doesn't mean—'

'Oh yes, it does,' Toby said. 'It means *rabbits*. The ones we created. Through the formicarium you gave us.' He crushed the head of yet another invading ant. '*Spiritual* rabbits,' he said, nastily.

Vinny said, 'Shut up, Toby. Let it drop.'

Aunt Craven said, 'I've had a hard day. I'm not in the

119

mood for impertinence. I don't expect you to respect my beliefs, but—'

'And we don't expect you to believe our facts,' Toby said.

'Very well, then,' Aunt Craven said. 'Have it your way. And I'll take back my marvellous, magical gift, which you think so little of, thank you very much.'

She grabbed the formicarium and strode from the room, carrying it.

Until this moment, Vinny had been apathetic. Now she ran after Aunt Craven. 'Don't break it!' she screamed. 'Whatever you do, don't let the Queen go!'

But Aunt Craven was already halfway up the stairs. 'Down the WC, that's where your precious ants are going!' she called.

Vinny scrambled after her – caught up with her – and cried, 'No! Don't! You don't understand!' She pushed her way past Aunt Craven, ran into the lavatory and sat down on the WC, glaring.

Aunt Craven stood over her. She began to laugh. 'If you could only see yourself!' she said. 'Queen Vinny on her throne!'

'Please, listen! It's all true about Mindbending! How can you be so stupid! If the Queen gets free—'

Aunt Craven's laughter ended. 'That's quite enough from you,' she said. She stepped forward, opened the small window and said, 'And that's quite enough of *you* too!'

With an expert backhand flip, she threw the formicarium out of the window.

Vinny heard it land and smash. She stared at Aunt Craven for a moment, then gave a single, short sob. 'You've done it now,' she said, despairingly. 'You've really done it now.'

Aunt Craven turned on her heel and clumped downstairs. Vinny slowly followed. She went to Toby.

'She's thrown them out of the window,' she said.

'Who's thrown what out? You don't mean—'

'Yes, I do. She threw the formicarium out of the window. I heard it smash.'

'But she can't do that! The Queen will get loose!'

'That's right. So the whole thing will start all over again. More eggs, more larvae and pupae, more giant ants.'

Toby said, almost in a whisper, 'There must be something we can do, Vinny.'

'There isn't. We're done for.'

'No, wait! Are you still hearing the Queen? The Voice?'

Vinny looked up with a flicker of hope in her eyes. 'Yes! Wait, I think so . . .'

'Couldn't the Voice lead us to her?'

'Don't talk. Let me concentrate.'

An ant had got its head and thorax through the gap in the window. Toby smashed the hoe at it. The ant wriggled, gaped and fell back. Another ant replaced it. He hit it with the hoe. Killing ants no longer sickened him. But the thought of the Queen at large, the thought of a town, a country, a continent, a whole world overrun by giant ants – that made him sick inside.

The Mother Queen said, 'Something has changed. My palace is in ruins! Everything is broken! What has happened to me?'

The Daughter Queen said, 'I don't understand, Your Majesty. You should just see *my* queendom! Everything spoilt—'

'Don't bother me with trifles. Are all your warriors free now? Are they all advancing?'

'They've nearly all freed themselves, yes. But it's terrible, everything's falling on our heads—'

'They are to advance! That is my command: advance, kill, conquer! Let there be no . . .'

Suddenly the Voice was silent.

'*Right*, you lot,' Greg said. 'Your turn now!' He pointed the Renault at a particular group of ants.

'Right!' Toby said. 'I'm going out there! I'm going to find the formicarium and jump on it! Smash the ants, smash the Queen! Let go of me, Vinny!'

'Advance, kill, conquer!' an ant repeated to itself. The command was never out of its head. It scuttled forward, gathered its strength and flung itself at the wall facing it. As it sprang, one of its legs, too weak to support the huge body, snapped. The ant bit off the dangling leg. 'Advance!' commanded the Voice. It tried to obey but could not. Infuriated, it swung its head and bit the ant next to it. There was a brief snapping of jaws. The crippled ant hobbled away, defeated. It vented its spite on some glittering stuff lying in the grass. The ant bit it: it bit back, it hurt. It was glass. There were little ants, tiny ants, among the glass fragments. The ant jerked its head at them, scooped them up and devoured them from sheer rage.

The Renault's tyres rolled and crushed.

Toby found the remains of the formicarium and stamped it into the ground.

The maddened giant ant, close at Toby's heels, scooped and mashed little ants with its jaws.

One way or another, the Mother Queen died.

At once, the battlefield became almost still.

Warrior ants still ran – but headed for nowhere. Ants attacking the windows still formed pyramids and clusters – but slowly, uncertainly, the shapes collapsed and the ants that formed them ran hither and thither without purpose.

Ants questioned each other by touching antennae, butting heads, squirting chemical messages. 'What? Why? Where now?' they asked each other. No answers came.

The Daughter Queen asked the same questions. But the Mother Queen was dead. There was no ruler, no Voice, to answer the questions; no will to issue commands.

* * *

Greg Stewkeley's workers arrived. The lights of their cars floodlit the house and its garden. Neighbours, attracted by the lights, arrived too. Spades, axes, improvised clubs – they all rose and fell, destroying the docile ants.

'Nasty looking creatures (thwack!),' said one man. 'But there's no (thwack!) vice in them, is there?'

'There's another lot over there,' said his neighbour. 'You take a rest, give me that shovel.' Thwack, thwack, thwack.

Robbie went from room to room of his house, making sure that no ants had got in. Bets made gallons of tea. Aunt Craven was outside, killing ants. As she worked, she hummed an old hymn tune: 'Bringing in the sheaves, bringing in the sheaves, we shall come rejoicing, bringing in the sheaves.'

Toby and Vinny stood looking down at a glittering, small mess on the lawn: the remains of the formicarium.

Toby said, 'What are you snivelling about?'

Vinny said, 'I don't know. I must be barmy.'

Chapter Eleven

Home was chaos. The house and garden no longer belonged to the family: complete strangers pushed past laying cables, setting up lights and cameras, forming queues to use the telephone, the lavatory, the kitchen. Until Robbie put his foot down, the tea kettle was never off the boil.

'Local press, national press, health authority, council, TV, local and national radio,' Toby said, gloomily. 'We're famous after all, Vin. Without having to do our act.'

'I just wish it was all over,' Vinny said.

Toby, alarmed, said, 'You don't mean you're still hearing the Voice, Vin?'

'No, I didn't mean that. I meant, I wish everyone would go and leave us in peace.'

'The Queen *is* dead, isn't she? Isn't she, Vinny?'

'She's dead. I heard her die.' Vinny shuddered.

'Then there's nothing to worry about, is there?' Toby asked.

'No. Of course not.'

A pretty, self-assured lady journalist approached Toby and Vinny, and said, '*Please* help, I've simply *got* to use the loo, I'm *bursting!* May I use the upstairs bathroom?' She put her head on one side and looked appealing.

Toby said, 'I've disconnected the upstairs 'phone. With this.' He showed her a small screwdriver.

The journalist's winning smile instantly faded. She snarled a single rude word and went away. 'She's about the tenth one to try that,' Toby told Vinny.

'Not a call of Nature, just a call,' Vinny said. She laughed for a second, but only a second. Her eyes were red-rimmed and exhausted. 'Why won't they all *go*?' she groaned. Then – 'Look at Greg! He's the hero . . .'

Greg seemed to be doing everything from tea-making to organizing the clearing away of dead ants. The bodies lay everywhere. Some still moved. A few got up and ran. These live ants were chased by photographers and people carrying spades and other weapons. The weapon-carriers shouted, 'Quick! Smash it!' and the photographers shouted, 'Wait! Don't touch it!' as they tried snatch a picture.

Greg kept everything going. Though it was dawn and cold, and everyone was tired, he radiated cheerfulness. 'Ha-*hard* down on your ri-*hight*,' he bellowed to the man driving the mini-tractor. 'Ster-*heady* as you go-ho!' The tractor had a scoop in front that shovelled bodies on to a great pile behind the house. The job was disgusting, but Greg kept the driver smiling.

Greg's secretary arrived in the Jaguar and said, 'Here they are, Mr Stewkeley. The stickers.'

'Ah. Good. Help me stick 'em on.'

The two of them unpeeled bright new king-sized adhesive labels and stuck them on each of the many items of equipment that Greg's team had brought. Greg dropped everything to work at this new task.

'What are those in aid of?' Toby asked.

'Advertising pays,' Greg answered, with a wink. 'Free advertising, right? Here – do us a favour – take this lot and stick them on the gear over there, where the TV cameras are.'

He thrust stickers into Toby's hands. They had big black lettering on a brilliant yellow background. They read:

LEKTRONIC
ENTERPRISES

Aunt Craven called, 'Pssst!' from the upstairs bathroom window. Toby and Vinny went to her. 'I've got to get *away!*' Aunt Craven said, urgently. '*Escape*, before they spot me!'

'Who, Aunt Craven? Why?'

'Don't be so *dim* – the newspaper people, of course! I'm supposed to be a *journalist* and here I am in the middle of the biggest story going, and I haven't even 'phoned in! All I've done is poke at ants with a hoe! You've got to smuggle me out!'

'But Aunt Craven—'

'If anyone sees me, my name will be *mud*. Go to that Stewkeley man. Tell him I must have my Daimler. Make him get someone to deliver it – put it where I can pick it up without being seen. Hurry.'

Vinny spoke to Greg. Greg spoke to Barry da Silva. Barry made some telephone calls. 'We'll have her Daimler parked in Marchmont Road in ten minutes,' Barry said. Vinny nodded. Marchmont Road would be deserted. 'Fifteen pounds delivery charge,' Barry said. 'Cash preferred.' Vinny nodded again.

'If anyone *sees* me, I'm done for!' Aunt Craven repeated, in a despairing hoot.

Vinny said, 'Hang on. Wig.'

She found the blonde wig her mother had used years ago, in an amateur-dramatics production. 'Sit here in front of the mirror, Aunt Craven. Don't move.' She pulled the wig down over Aunt Craven's head.

However she adjusted it, the wig was not a success. It was brazen yellow with a flirty fringe. It did not seem to suit Aunt Craven's stern, miserable face. And when Vinny tugged at the wig, strands of long blonde hair came away. This made Aunt Craven's face grimmer

128

and more miserable than ever. Yet Vinny did not laugh even once.

'Lipstick, Aunt Craven,' Vinny said. 'I mean, with hair like that, you have to lash on plenty of lipstick.'

'This one might do,' Toby gravely suggested. He handed Vinny his mother's brightest, reddest lipstick. He too had managed not to laugh. He did not even smile when Aunt Craven's determined mouth became a scarlet wound. He just said, 'Shiny high heels, don't you think?'

They smuggled her out of the house and made for Marchmont Road. It was a difficult journey. Aunt Craven was not used to high heels. The only shoes that seemed to go with the blonde wig and the lipstick had very high heels. They wobbled. So did the wig.

To save time, Toby went ahead with Aunt Craven's suitcases. They were awkward and heavy. He sweated and got into a bad temper.

Just as he was loading the cases into the boot of the Daimler, he saw Vinny coming towards him accompanied by an extraordinary woman, obviously staggering-drunk.

It took Toby several seconds to realize that this drunken woman was Aunt Craven. When he did realize it, he began laughing. He laughed so hard that he draped himself over the rear of the Daimler, crying, 'That wig . . . that mouth . . . those shoe-hoo-hoos . . .'

Vinny, determined not to laugh, started counting up to twenty. At seventeen, however, something inside gave way and a burst of laughter forced its way past her throat. She laughed so much that she got cramp in her side and had to sit on the tarmac, bent double.

All this time, Aunt Craven had been making small, furious sounds: groans, muffled oaths or loud gasps when her high heels buckled under her. Scowling, she tottered to clutch at a wing mirror – caught a glimpse of herself in it – leaned forward to take a closer look – and she too started laughing. She began quite quietly. She ended helpless, with her wig over one eye. She clung to Toby for support and laughed till she cried.

Three minutes later, the departing Daimler showed its dignified backside and Toby and Vinny were alone, wiping their eyes and rubbing their aching sides. 'Well . . .,' Vinny managed to say, 'she's gone.'

'It's all right, she'll be back,' Toby said.

'You sound as if you're glad,' Vinny said, surprised.

'Why shouldn't I be glad?' Toby said, raising one eyebrow loftily. 'Aunt Craven's *all right*. I always said so.'

'I give up,' Vinny said.

They walked home. Cars and vans rushed past them, all heading in the same direction – away from home.

'They're leaving,' Vinny said. 'Thank goodness.'

It was surprising, really, how quickly the giant ants were forgotten: how soon things got back to normal. 'It's as if nothing had ever happened,' Bets said. 'Nothing in the papers for days. Nothing on TV.'

'Merciful oblivion,' Robbie said.

'But it was exciting,' Toby said. 'Us being right at the centre of it all ... What are you pulling faces for, Vinny?'

'I hated it, I hated *them*,' Vinny said, in a low, violent voice.

'You two bring dinner things into the kitchen,' Bets said over her shoulder. She and Robbie carried out plates and dishes. Toby and Vinny were alone. Toby said, 'There's no need to get all uptight about it. It's over. And anyhow, I thought you wanted to be a Mental Magic star, the child wonder and everything.'

'I don't want anything like that now. Now or ever.'

'You mean, you don't ever want to give Mental Magic another go? Why ever not? Just because it went a bit wrong with the ants—'

'A *bit* wrong!' she exploded. 'It could have been a world disaster!'

'Well, it wasn't. The ants lost, we won and all the bodies have been cleared from the battlefield. I bet if we tried again with the old Mindbending, we could—'

'We couldn't,' Vinny said. 'No formicarium, no Mental Magic.'

'How do you know that?' Toby asked, suspiciously. 'Have you been doing a bit of Mindbending on the quiet?'

She did not answer. She got up and ran to her room. Bets and Robbie came back from the kitchen. 'You two were supposed to help clear the table,' Bets said. 'Where's Vinny disappeared to? Take out those glasses and the butter, Toby. Craven's on in five minutes.'

'Oh! That's right!' Toby said. 'On the box. Great. I'll get Vinny.' He cleared the things off the table at high speed, then ran upstairs. 'Vinny!' he said. 'Aunt Craven's on TV any moment now!' He looked into her face and said, 'What's up?'

'Nothing's up.'

'Yes there is, you've got that look on your face. Anyhow, come downstairs and watch the Aunt.'

Just as the programme began, the front doorbell rang and Toby had to answer it. 'Greg Stewkeley,' he announced.

'Oh, come in, Mr Stewkeley,' Bets said. 'Do you mind if we watch this? It's my sister Craven.'

'Great lady, your sister,' Greg said, and sat down. 'I just dropped by to let you have Barry da Silva's final account for her Daimler—'

'The programme's starting.'

Science Q & A flashed up on the screen, and there she was: Aunt Craven, with three other scientific people and a self-assured presenter who kept interrupting.

'She's even bossier than Aunt Craven!' Toby whispered. 'There'll be trouble!'

The trouble came when the panel of scientists started discussing mutations: how living things change to meet changing circumstances. The presenter turned to Aunt

Craven and said, 'But you have actually observed a dramatic mutation at close quarters, haven't you?'

'Don't want to talk about it,' Aunt Craven said, gruffly.

'Oh, but surely! We've been led to believe that you are uniquely qualified to tell us about an almost *mystical* mutation? The giant ants?'

'Mystical, my eye,' Aunt Craven said, indistinctly.

The presenter pounced. 'Ah. I see. Well, if it *wasn't* mystical . . ?'

'Very complicated story,' Aunt Craven bumbled. 'Many possible causes, including a rather mysterious—'

'But not *mystical?*' insisted the presenter.

Aunt Craven went into a long and involved attempt to explain what she meant, and ended by saying she didn't mean it anyway.

'Poor Aunt Craven,' Robbie said, when Aunt Craven at last dried up. 'What a mess she got herself into.' He was really upset.

Greg said, 'Well, she had her reasons, didn't she?'

'What do you mean?' Toby asked him.

'You know what I mean,' Greg said. 'The ants and everything: sort of a *family* affair, wasn't it?' He looked hard at Vinny and Toby, then switched on his smile and said, 'Must be going.'

'What *did* Greg mean?' Toby asked Vinny later.

Vinny said, 'Aunt Craven didn't want to drag us into

the giant ant thing. She knows – and *I* know, and *you* know – that we were the cause of it all.'

'And Greg knows too?' Toby asked. He gave a low whistle. 'Ouch!' he said. 'I suppose he'll be after us to start Mindbending again. With him as business manager.'

'Of course. But we won't. Because we can't, as I've already told you. No giant ants, no formicarium, no Mental Magic.'

'You sound very sure,' Toby said. Bloggs jumped on to his lap. He stroked the cat's head. Bloggs set up a low, rumbling purr. Toby could feel it as well as hear it. Lovely.

A wave of contentment flowed over him. Suddenly he no longer wanted to become a star of screen, stage and TV. He no longer wanted money and the things it could buy. He just wanted what he already had. Including old Bloggs, purring away to himself. He wanted to be like Bloggs.

'Oh well,' he said to Vinny. 'It's all over now. Over and done with.' He smiled at his sister.

'Over and done with,' Vinny said. She did not smile back.

'Over and done with,' Vinny told herself as she lay in bed that night. Well, it was true. The council and health authority workers had made a thorough job of wiping out the ants' nest beneath the fallen tree. Poisons, gas, an excavator. They had even removed the tree.

No giant ants could possibly survive in the site of the nest, or anywhere near it.

Vinny no longer heard the Voice of the Mother Queen.

Over and done with.

She lay rigid, eyes clenched shut. Sleep! she told herself.

Seven miles away, a Labrador called Prince trotted across the common. Prince's master always took the dog for a walk after dinner. The master threw a ball and Prince rushed after it.

'Fetch it, Prince!' The ball went up in the night air, disappearing into the darkness. But Prince could smell and hear the ball when it fell; and off he went, paws pounding and tail waving. 'Bring it back, Prince!'

But the ball had bounced into a thicket. Prince had to fight his way to it. There it was! Its smell was unmistakable. Prince grinned and followed his nose.

There was another smell, not friendly, not familiar, an unknown smell, a stink. Prince paused.

And then there was a Thing. It was big and shining, it moved towards him in quick jerks, it had teeth, it wanted to fight!

Prince yelped, backed away and went back to his master with his tail down. 'Where's the ball, Prince? Go on, boy! Fetch! Bring me the ball!'

But Prince would not leave his master's side.

*   *   *

Vinny could not sleep, her mind would not let go of her. Just when she was dropping off, her mind jolted her awake with small, meaningless, unwanted snatches of thought, or talk, or something.

'*So difficult without her,*' said the voice in her mind.

'*I'm not like she was, just not good at decisions,*' it said.

'*So few of us left,*' it said.

'*All the same, I suppose there are enough,*' it said, uncertainly.

'*I'm sure there are enough!*' it said, much more confidently.

Two more chilling paranormal adventures by

Nicholas Fisk

Something strange is out there ... Only ordinary children, with astonishing paranormal powers, can find out what it is ...

TRILLIONS

A layer of hard, shiny dust covers the village of Harbourtown. The Trillions have landed. But what are they? Where have they come from? In the race to find the answers, the experts are baffled. Only one boy has the power to discover the truth. And stop a deadly invasion – before it's too late ...

FLIP SIDE

Lettice has always had a special bond with animals – she's forever talking to her pets. Is this simply a natural rapport? Or is it something deeper? When a world catastrophe threatens and animals everywhere are thrown into chaos, Lettice needs all her powers of communication to save the world from a deadly invasion ...

ORDER FORM

Nicholas Fisk

71021 7	TRILLIONS	£3.99	❏
71019 5	FLIP SIDE	£3.99	❏

All Hodder Children's books are available at your local bookshop or newsagent, or can be ordered direct from the publisher. Just tick the titles you want and fill in the form below. Prices and availability subject to change without notice.

Hodder Children's Books, Cash Sales Department, Bookpoint, 39 Milton Park, Abingdon, OXON, OX14 4TD, UK. If you have a credit card you may order by telephone – (01235) 400414.

Please enclose a cheque or postal order made payable to Bookpoint Ltd to the value of the cover price and allow the following for postage and packing:
UK & BFPO – £1.00 for the first book, 50p for the second book, and 30p for each additional book ordered up to a maximum charge of £3.00.
OVERSEAS & EIRE – £2.00 for the first book, £1.00 for the second book, and 50p for each additional book.

Name..

Address..

....

....

If you would prefer to pay by credit card, please complete:
Please debit my Visa/Access/Diner's Card/American Express (delete as applicable) card no:

Signature..

Expiry Date..